Lucy Crisp

AND THE

VANISHING HOUSE

Lucy Crisp

AND THE
VANISHING HOUSE

JANET HILL

tundra

For my husband, John,
who puts up with a lot

Text and illustrations copyright © 2020 by Janet Hill

Tundra Books, an imprint of Penguin Random House Canada Young Readers,
a Penguin Random House Company

Library and Archives Canada Cataloguing in Publication

Title: Lucy Crisp and the vanishing house / Janet Hill
Names: Hill, Janet, 1974- author.
Identifiers: Canadiana (print) 20190148500 | Canadiana (ebook) 20190148519 |
ISBN 9781770499249 (hardcover) | ISBN 9781770499256 (EPUB)
Classification: LCC PS8615.I4173 L83 2020 | DDC jC813/.6—dc23

Published simultaneously in the United States of America by Tundra Books of
Northern New York, an imprint of Penguin Random House Canada Young Readers,
a Penguin Random House Company

Library of Congress Control Number: 2019944756

Acquired by Tara Walker
Edited by Elizabeth Kribs
Designed by Kelly Hill
The artwork in this book was rendered in oil on canvas.
The text was set in Adobe Caslon Pro.

Printed and bound in China

www.penguinrandomhouse.ca

1 2 3 4 5   24 23 22 21 20

Penguin
Random House
tundra | TUNDRA BOOKS

"In the picturesque Finger Lakes region of New York State, there is a town called Esther Wren. It is a quiet place with wide, leafy streets; painstakingly preserved heritage homes; and quaint shops selling peanut brittle and postcards. Yet, beneath the town's sanguine surface, mystery finds its definition. Rose gardens are self-tended, yard sales are hazardous to one's health, and stately white houses disappear like sugar cubes stirred into black coffee."

CLEMENTINE HOWARD,
witch theorist, *A Beginner's Guide to Witches*

CHAPTER ONE

Roses

Lucy tied the white apron around her waist and anxiously waited for her next instruction. It was her first day on the job, and so far the only thing she had managed to grasp was how to avoid being trampled on. The flower shop was a beehive of activity with deliveries, phone calls, and a steady stream of customers picking up their cedar garlands, poinsettias, and artfully asymmetrical wreaths. But what concerned Lucy the most were the three florist apprentices with their topknots and flowy kimono blouses who whirled around the shopfront displays with such speed and agility it made her feel almost motion sick.

"Come with me. I'll show you the workroom." An apprentice suddenly appeared by Lucy's side and grabbed her by the wrist, navigating her safely around browsing customers, past a wall of humming coolers, and then down a pale-green hallway. "You'll be spending a lot of time back here, especially during wedding prep. I hope you know how to work a mop."

Cold air nipped at Lucy's bare arms when they stepped inside the workroom to discover Ivy, the aptly named florist, laboriously working on an elaborate Christmas-themed centerpiece of mossy birch branches and ivory roses.

"Never touch anything on that desk." The apprentice pointed toward a wooden desk smothered in stacks of invoices, a phone with a cracked screen, and the remnants of a bran muffin and coffee. "And never use that phone. It's only for our suppliers."

Ivy had momentarily diverted her attention away from the centerpiece to give Lucy a quick smile when suddenly the phone rang. The two women exchanged a tense look.

"They said they would call today. You'd better get it. I might lose my patience with them," Ivy said.

The apprentice answered the call while Ivy drew in a breath so sharp it seemed to suck all the air out of the room. The conversation was brief and mostly one-sided, and as soon as the apprentice hung up, Ivy pounced on her.

"How many?"

"Eighteen hundred."

"That's it?"

"That's it."

"That means only a hundred and fifty bouquets. No one on the waiting list will get one this year."

"Looks like." The apprentice sighed. "I'll start calling people."

"Any word about the shades?"

"They don't know yet."

"When's the delivery date?"

"They said they couldn't give an exact date—only that it will be next month sometime. You know how they work—they'll let us know once they're on the road."

"Oh for God's sake." Ivy sighed, then turned her attention back to the centerpiece.

"Follow me and I'll show you the loading dock," the apprentice instructed Lucy. "Remember to watch the gap between the door and the dock. It's a broken ankle just waiting to happen."

The "gap." Lucy tensed at hearing the word spoken out loud, like a curse tossed into a pleasant conversation for no apparent reason. It was an unwelcome reminder that she was technically halfway through her second gap year, after her first failed to yield positive results. Her time of freedom and self-discovery had been squandered in an equal mix of waitressing and entry-level office jobs. Her lowest point was a two-day stint as a dog walker that ended abruptly when she was bitten by a bad-tempered bichon frise called Whoopsie Daisy while cleaning up after a greyhound that had eaten a bowl of lamb curry. Unable to afford a place of her own, Lucy lived in New York City with her father, a food writer and restaurant critic who had an insatiable appetite for both food and entertaining. Their prewar apartment was the perfect venue for his parties with its generously proportioned living and dining spaces—where most of the activity centered around two velvet sofas with fraying arms and a wine-stained pine dining table that could seat twelve in a pinch. Lucy's refuge from the revolving door of dinner parties and wine tastings was to hide in her bedroom with her nose buried

in a book. Lately, she had been coveting old paperback mysteries, the kind where clues were cleverly concealed in plain sight like a sleight-of-hand card trick in a magic show.

Lucy's history of unsteady employment had led to her involuntary position of unpaid errand girl for her father. Several days a week she was given a complex grocery list that usually consisted of at least one unattainable item—typically a rare Welsh cheese or an unpronounceable spice. Her visits to various shops and bakeries were so frequent that she had gotten to know many of the owners and employees by name, and it was while picking up a centerpiece arrangement for her father's latest social gathering that she noticed the *Help Wanted* sign in the window of the flower shop. Although the job was temporary (to assist during the holiday rush), Lucy didn't mind, since the month of December only meant an increase in her father's parties, which she was more than happy to avoid.

It didn't take Lucy long to find her place in the shop amid all the hustle and bustle. She was a quick study and learned how to predict the apprentices' sudden movements and which customers needed a little extra care. She survived the weekly wedding preparations while maintaining a cool head even with the most tempestuous of brides. Sometimes at the end of the day, Lucy found herself creating pretty posies from the discarded flower clippings and bringing them home to decorate the dining table. Her ability to conquer any task tossed at her had impressed the florist so much that she was asked to stay on until Valentine's Day.

The day when "the gap" had begun to close was the same day the flower shop received a very special delivery of roses—so special that Ivy made sure she was present for their arrival and oversaw every aspect of their handling. They were referred to as the Ladywyck Variety—available exclusively during the month of January and discussed in only the most hushed and reverent of tones amongst the florist and her apprentices. Lucy immediately understood that these particular flowers had been the subject of the mysterious phone call on her first day of work.

The roses came in seven shades: Cream Tea, Smoke Mauve, Summer Lemons, Exquisite Pink, Silversmith, Marmalady, and Crowning Royal Red, and every single flower was perfection—from the silken soft petals right down to the glossy dark-green stem. Ivy and her apprentices worked elbow to elbow for the rest of the day in a fragrant fog of cloves and vanilla that had made Lucy hungry for dessert.

Once all the Ladywyck roses had been tied in bunches with French-velvet ribbon, wrapped in ivory tissue paper, placed into long gold boxes, and hand delivered to the most discerning of New York's rose connoisseurs, Lucy sat down on the edge of the loading dock to enjoy the last sips of her lukewarm coffee. Ivy sat down beside her and released a long and satisfied yawn.

"Ladywyck roses have a lengthy life. There's nothing else like them."

"Are they genetically modified or something?" Lucy asked.

Ivy smiled coyly. "I guess you've never heard of Ladywyck Lodge?"

"Is that the farm where they're grown?"

"Not a farm exactly—more of an arts college. But they do have large gardens and greenhouses where they grow the most wonderful flowers and vegetables. Mostly they offer culinary classes, writing workshops, painting, printmaking, flower arranging. That kind of thing." Ivy paused. "You should apply for one of their floristry workshops. Those posies that you create from leftover cuttings are quite darling—they show real potential. Never mind your knack for sentiment cards. Most people stare at them for ages trying to think of something clever or witty to say before they eventually surrender to the standard 'Thinking of You' or 'Happy Birthday.' But you always come up with the most ingenious of phrases. That little poem you wrote for the woman with the sick niece about the cowgirl and the unicorn was brilliant. With some proper training and a few years of apprenticeship under your belt, I can see you owning your own flower shop one day."

Lucy had never considered owning her own business before, but she did find the idea appealing. The flower shop had awakened her creativity—not only with designing her own arrangements, but also with her imagination. There were so many stories behind their deliveries—like the elderly gentleman who ordered a violet nosegay every week for an ex-burlesque dancer named Violette Storm whom he had been pursuing since 1963. When placing his last order he had victoriously announced that she had finally agreed to dinner and a show. It was a first date fifty years in the making. Or the woman who sheepishly placed orders for a dozen red roses to be sent to herself at her office, which Lucy had quickly understood was done in an effort to make a coworker jealous. Not to mention the strange elderly lady who sent her sister's dog Lulu white lilies every other Wednesday.

"Just a second," Ivy said. She went inside and returned a moment later holding a yellow rose. "They always include a few extra."

Lucy accepted the rose as if it were made of fine crystal.

"Watch out—they still have their thorns. Never strip a Ladywyck rose of its thorns or you will strip it of its life. Change the water daily and it should last at least three months," the florist said before returning inside.

Lucy twirled the rose between her fingertips while she daydreamed a future filled with flowers. When a sharp pain brought her back to the present, she looked down to see a tiny bead of blood on her thumb.

CHAPTER TWO

Snowflakes

Lucy kept the yellow rose in an ordinary juice glass on her bedside table, where for the past several weeks she observed it for any signs of wilting or decay. But the only change in its appearance was the languid unfurling of petals that released a sweet, almost cinnamon-like fragrance. Lucy had also noticed that the rose was thirstier than any other flower she'd ever encountered—requiring at least a cup of water a day. Its unusual nature deepened Lucy's curiosity about its origins, and it wasn't long before she found herself navigating the Ladywyck Lodge website. Although the site was outdated, with just a handful of photographs, Lucy felt drawn to the mysterious school. There were beekeeping classes and mermaid mythology lectures and a whole other curriculum available only to students with special membership. The floral artistry program was a year in length, and in order to apply, she had to submit a portfolio consisting of ten photographs of her own arrangements and a brief essay about herself. With a little guidance from Ivy and her apprentices, Lucy created a series of hand-tied bouquets fitting for an aspiring florist of her experience. Once her portfolio was complete and the stamps were licked, Lucy watched as her application tumbled into the black hole of the mailbox. Then she convinced herself that she no longer cared and put it out of her mind.

Lucy's job at the flower shop ended the day after Valentine's Day with a promise that she would be called back for Easter and Mother's Day. In the meantime, she had decided to help out a friend who was preparing to launch a gourmet nut business (ironically nut- and gluten-free) at a local pop-up market. After a sleet-soaked Saturday that yielded no sales, Lucy's friend reneged on her eight-dollar-an-hour wage arrangement and Lucy once again felt the gap widen.

That was until an unremarkable gray morning in late March when a registered letter arrived for Lucy just as she was making coffee. In the upper-left corner there was a lithographed design of a herd of cows above the words *LADYWYCK LODGE*, printed in an Olde-English-style script. Silence engulfed the room and Lucy felt her arms bloom with goose bumps. For several seconds she clutched the letter, trying to envision the contents and convince herself that she still didn't care either way. Then the coffee pot percolated loudly, and a siren wailed nearby, and Lucy tore the top off the envelope and unfolded the paper. Her eyes latched onto one word: *Congratulations!*

"Oh good, you made coffee." Lucy's father walked into the room carrying a bag of groceries from his morning jog to the market.

Startled, Lucy leapt to her feet.

"French press?" he asked hopefully.

"No, sorry. Just regular."

"Have you had breakfast yet?"

"Not yet."

"Feel like an omelette?"

"I was about to go out for some avocado toast."

"Oh no. Don't do that. Haven't you heard about the illegal defor-estation?" Lucy's father said while removing his wet windbreaker.

"Can't say I have." Lucy sighed as she prepared herself for another lecture on willful ignorance.

"You live in a bubble. You can't just turn your back on important news."

"Sometimes it's not news; it's just too much information," Lucy said as she realized she hadn't touched her phone in almost a week.

"Well, it's a disgrace. They're tearing down forests so they can plant avocados—all because of this ridiculous hipster trend. How about I make you a brie and mushroom omelette instead?"

Lucy's focus had returned to the letter. Her father took her silence for compliance and began to set the table. "You got some mail?"

"It's an acceptance letter," Lucy replied.

"Really? From where?" he asked, his voice rising with excitement.

"Ladywyck Lodge."

"You got accepted to Ladywyck Lodge?"

"You know about Ladywyck?"

"Of course! All the best restaurants trip over themselves trying to get their hands on Ladywyck's produce. Do you remember that time I had those fiddleheads in brown butter that I couldn't stop talking about for a year?"

"How could I forget? You wrote a three-page article about those fiddleheads."

"Well, those came from Ladywyck. What program were you accepted into?"

"Floral artistry. It's a one-year certificate program. If I complete it, I'll get hired on as full-time apprentice at the flower shop."

Lucy's father's face fell.

"Is that what you want? To be a florist?"

"Do you have a better idea? It's been almost two years of searching and this is the only job I haven't hated."

Lucy's father took off his glasses and wearily rubbed his eyes.

"Is that really how you should be choosing your future career? If you don't hate it, then it's meant to be?" he asked, sweeping aside a stack of sauce-stained cookbooks from the center of the table.

"Well, I'm never going to be an accountant or a lawyer or a stockbroker. So no matter what I choose, you won't approve," Lucy said sharply.

"That's not true. I just wanted things to be easier for you than they were for me. It was years and years of struggle—"

"I know, Dad. You don't have to remind me about the clothes frozen to the radiator and the phone down the hall and the time you had to eat an onion for breakfast because there was nothing else in the cupboard. You've told me a million times."

"I just want you to pursue a career that's a little more

straightforward. Never underestimate a steady income, pension, and benefits. Do you have any idea how expensive dental work is? Besides, you never really showed much of an interest in flowers before working at that shop."

Lucy knew that he wasn't entirely wrong.

"Look at it this way. If people keep marrying and dying then I will always have a steady income."

Lucy's father couldn't argue with that statement.

"Well, if you were accepted to Ladywyck, then at the very least, it merits a visit."

The following week, Lucy and her father drove four hours upstate to take a tour of the lodge. They arrived in Esther Wren on the heels of a blustery snowstorm that tapered to a gentle snowfall the moment they entered the town. With a few minutes to spare before their appointment, they decided to take the lakeside route through the historic district and soak in the local atmosphere. Lucy's father became giddy at the sight of a main street lined with one-of-a-kind shops, including an old-fashioned hardware store still wearing its Christmas decorations. After a few blocks, the shops gave way to houses, all distinguished and old, and each one different from the next. Some even had turrets and stained glass, and probably a ghost or two. All the while, the snow continued to fall, melting on the windshield and leaving Lucy with the feeling of being comforted somehow, as though she was looking into a gently shaken snow globe.

At the lodge they were greeted by a woman in her sixties. "Hello, I'm Helen, one of Ladywyck's guardians." Helen was petite with hair the color of pink cotton candy, and she was dressed entirely in black except for an armful of vintage Bakelite bracelets. She smiled warmly at Lucy. "You know, arriving during a snowstorm is a good omen. 'No snowflake ever falls in the wrong place.'"

Before beginning the tour, Helen asked Lucy and her father to turn off their phones and any other wireless devices they might have brought with them. She explained that they liked to keep the energy surrounding the lodge clean and free from interference. Lucy's father appeared visibly pained as he reached into his coat pocket to turn his off, while Lucy realized she'd forgotten hers at home.

The tour included the entire first floor, greenhouses, gardens, orchards, and the conservatory, where most of Lucy's time would be spent. On the way to view the winter gardens, Lucy's heart fluttered at the sight of warm lights emanating from the windows of the tiny cabins sprinkled across the property, which Helen explained were reserved as work spaces for the students enrolled in the creative writing program. After the tour, Helen, Lucy, and Lucy's father sat by the crackling fire with cups of cinnamon tea and warm apple tarts and pored over the curriculum outline. Floristry students were also encouraged to explore their artistic side with painting, sculpture, and art history classes. Lucy could sense that her father was less than impressed with the course descriptions, which included Introduction to Ornamental Grasses and Boutonnieres for Beginners. He asked about the type of accreditation his daughter would receive upon graduation, and Helen explained that while she would receive a certificate, what Ladywyck considered of greater importance was that Lucy would be fulfilling her destiny. Lucy's father raised his eyebrows at Lucy before scraping the plate clean of his apple tart.

The school provided no on-site lodging for students, so Helen recommended that Lucy rent an apartment or room in town. To get a feel for prices and availability, Lucy and her father headed downtown to the real estate office. As they were about to make their way inside, a house listing displayed front and center on the window caught their attention.

"Wow! It's like something out of a magazine," Lucy said.

"That can't be right," her father said excitedly as he pointed at the list price.

"Well, it's not the city, I guess."

"The photo is from the spring—look, the lilac tree is in bloom. How old is this listing?"

"Maybe it's already sold and they just forgot to take it down. Or maybe it's bait that they use to lure unsuspecting property-starved New Yorkers inside," Lucy joked.

Just then, Lucy noticed a pair of black eyes watching them from the other side of the window. Then she heard tapping on the glass, and a long tobacco-stained finger with red nails gestured for them to come inside.

The black eyes belonged to Millicent Brown, who immediately thrust a business card at Lucy and her father that read *Millicent Brown. The Only Realtor in Town.* As it turned out, that was not an exaggeration; Millicent owned the only real estate office in Esther Wren. She was quick to inform them that the house was not only still available

but also vacant, and she insisted on taking them on a tour. When they pulled up outside the house in Millicent's great white Cadillac, Lucy's jaw and her father's dropped simultaneously. There it stood in its winter version—wedding-cake white, on top of a blanket of freshly fallen snow that resembled icing sugar.

"Make no mistake, she's a looker," Millicent Brown growled proudly as she turned the engine off.

The house was indeed a "looker." It exuded character in all of its architectural details—from the mansard roof and tower to the exterior flourishes that included bracketing and gingerbread. It was also spacious: three stories tall, with high ceilings, wide-plank pine floors, and large windows of old glass that made Lucy feel as if she were staring through ripples of water. As far as Lucy was concerned the house's only flaw was the dowdy decorating—old-fashioned in style and in varying shades of brown, maroon, and mustard. She imagined it as a beautiful woman wearing an unflattering dress.

"A little spit and polish is all this grand old lady needs," Millicent said, rapping her fist against the staircase banister before she lit a cigarette and recited the history of the house.

"The house was built in 1876 by Captain Reginald Quill, a merchant sea captain who retired after a cholera epidemic had taken the lives of his crew. The sea was a painful reminder to him of that fateful voyage, and so he moved inland to our quiet town of Esther Wren, pouring his heart into his new home. It is a fine home, a pinnacle example of Second Empire architecture. In the last ten years of Captain Quill's life, he found solace in working with his hands, perfecting the interior of his home with fine moldings and generous woodwork, as you can see. He also occasionally made furniture, including children's toys, rocking horses, and the like for . . . children in need."

Lucy couldn't help but notice how the words "children in need" got caught in Millicent's throat and tossed out in one great smoky cough.

Once Lucy's father was convinced that the house was structurally sound—free from rot and asbestos—and that the neighborhood was safe, Millicent allotted them a few minutes to discuss the house in private. Lucy could tell by her father's wide eyes and rapid speaking that he was as besotted with the house as she was. But for him, it wasn't entirely about looks; it was about a good investment. And for the first time, Lucy didn't feel inclined to criticize his extravagant spending, since every bone in her body was telling her this is where she needed to be.

"But are you sure this is what you really want?" her father said. He paced back and forth, the floorboards quaintly creaking beneath his feet. "To move to a tiny town in the middle of nowhere—away from everyone and everything that you know—to study Boutonnieres for Beginners?"

Lucy nodded. "I can't quite explain it, but there's just something about this place. It feels right."

"Well, they do seem to embrace your old-fashioned ways, particularly with technology. What was that business about keeping the air clean from interference?"

"Maybe it's a health thing—or maybe they're just superstitious. Not everyone shares your Twitter addiction. But are you sure you can

afford this? I can just rent a studio apartment or something." The last words felt like a balloon deflating.

"It would mean putting the restaurant on hold for a little longer, but real estate is a much safer investment than a restaurant. It's as much for me as it is for you."

Lucy's father had been talking about opening his own restaurant for years, and Lucy suspected that this house purchase might also serve as a well-timed excuse to put off potential failure.

"Even though it's cheap, we will have to get you a housemate, or two, or five," her father joked. "But I'm sure the lodge can help to put us in touch with other students who need a place to stay."

And without giving it a further thought, Lucy's father tossed the real estate agent an offer that was so low it made her eyebrows lift to her hairline. She responded with a loud chortle from deep within her smokestack lungs, which Lucy interpreted to be an equal mix of admiration and disgust. She reached into her handbag and retrieved something that at first glance looked like a beige brick but turned out to be her phone—possibly the first cellphone ever manufactured, and excused herself to the privacy of the kitchen to make a call. She returned less than five minutes later and, with a grimace, delivered the good news that their offer was accepted.

On their way back to the car, Lucy's father started in on a one-sided conversation with Millicent about his daughter's acceptance to Ladywyck Lodge's floral artistry program. It was the first time he'd expressed pride about her acceptance—an attitude change that Lucy attributed to the excitement over his spontaneous house purchase. Millicent continued to walk at a brisk pace down the front path toward her Cadillac, ignoring him until she reached the sidewalk, where she informed them that she would require him to sign all the paperwork back at her office. Lucy's father climbed into the front seat, and just as Lucy was about to get in the car, Millicent gave her the side-eye and drew in one last puff of her cigarette.

"Artistic expression is the bowel movement of the mind," she said flatly before flicking her cigarette into the snow, where it extinguished with a desultory sizzle.

CHAPTER THREE

Visitors

O n a warm spring day in early May, Lucy and her father arrived at her new home. The rented van had barely come to a complete stop before Lucy leapt out of the passenger's seat, eager to explore every inch of the property. A feeling of relief washed over her when she saw that it looked just as it had in the listing photo at the real estate office—right down to the blooming lilac tree. While her father unpacked the first load of boxes, Lucy toured the gardens, admiring all the shrubs and plants that had been buried beneath a foot of snow the last time she'd been here. She walked up the front steps, and as she reached into her purse to retrieve the keys, she noticed an old-fashioned typewriter sitting on the front porch.

"Looks like an old Underwood," her father said as he trailed behind her balancing several boxes of kitchen supplies.

"Is it valuable?" Lucy asked.

"Not particularly. But that one appears to be in really good shape."

"I wonder what it's doing here," Lucy said, bending down to examine it more closely. "There's no note or anything."

"Maybe it's a housewarming gift from our friendly real estate agent. We know how much she appreciates the arts. Why don't you bring it inside? I'm sure we'll get to the bottom of it soon enough."

After spending the weekend getting Lucy settled in her new home, her father returned to the city, leaving his daughter with a lengthy list of chores to complete over the summer. Immediately she began hanging curtains, stripping wallpaper, and tending to the garden. Lengthy emails—dramatically titled "Garden Hose Hell," "Invasion of the Ants!" and "Mysterious Kitchen Cupboard Stench"—were exchanged between Lucy and her father on a daily basis. One of the more gratifying chores involved gathering up all the spare bits of staid Victorian furniture left behind by the previous owners and sending them off to auction. She did hold on to the portrait of Captain Quill, but she removed him from his spot above the fireplace mantel and tucked him away in a far corner in the attic, apologizing profusely as she covered him with an old cotton sheet.

In the growing heat of the afternoons, Lucy flexed her fledgling florist muscles by creating simple bouquets of spring flowers freshly cut from her garden. But increasingly, she found herself distracted by the old typewriter. At first it was more of a curiosity than anything else. She liked the vintage look of it and the sound of the keys as they clicked down, sealing an inky black letter onto the crisp white paper. But after a while, Lucy found herself not just typing but writing, and within a week she'd composed a quirky short story called "Lilies for

Lulu," which gave her an odd feeling of relief—like a confession she'd gotten off her chest.

The quiet was a luxury Lucy had rarely experienced. There were no sirens or heavy traffic sounds. No muffled voices or strange bangs and clangs could be heard through her walls and ceiling. There were the typical suburban daytime sounds of lawn mowers and car radios, but those were steeped in nostalgia and a comfort to Lucy. Then, every so often, there were the night noises carried across rooftops and into her bedroom just as she was falling asleep. They were wholly unfamiliar and hard to distinguish, but softly melodic and mysterious. They made her feel like a young girl going to bed early while the adults were still awake.

In spite of the solitude, Lucy wasn't lonely. She was so preoccupied with settling into her new home that she hadn't had a chance to realize that she'd hardly spoken to anyone with the exception of her next-door neighbor, who had approached her while she was pruning the lilac bush. Her name was Brenda Merriweather and she had a young daughter named Marigold, who clung shyly to her side while hugging her stuffed rabbit named Handsome. On the other side, in a rambling, painted Queen Anne, lived a family with four girls, all close in age and almost identical in appearance. Lucy had nicknamed them the French Braids, as they were all slender with bony knees and wore their tawny-colored hair in loose French braids. Most of their after-school time was spent on the front lawn reading books and writing in journals. On hotter days, they retreated to the shade of their front porch where they played with a collection of old canning jars. From the edge of her property, Lucy had attempted to see the

contents of the jars, but she could only make out that they were cloudy, bordering on murky—some even pitch-black. On occasion, one would flicker brightly like a candle, which made Lucy wonder if they contained fireflies or possibly glowworms.

One morning Lucy woke up a little earlier than usual and headed downstairs to the kitchen to make a pot of coffee. She had a busy day planned that involved cleaning up the greenhouse as well as composing another email to her dad. This one would be titled "Chimney Critter!" as she'd she spent a good part of the previous evening listening to the scratching sounds of at least one uninvited rodent. Following her usual path to the kitchen through the living room, she was stopped in her tracks by a chair in the middle of the room, a chair that hadn't been there the night before. Lucy approached the chair as she would approach a large dog she didn't know—slowly and with caution. It was tilted a little to the right, as if one of the legs was shorter than the others, and it was upholstered in a thin cotton fabric patterned with little bunnies and bunches of orange carrots. There was a ruffled skirt around the seat and the fraying fabric was crudely stapled at the seams. Lucy circled the chair several times over, then got down on her hands and knees and examined the underside, hoping to locate the manufacturer's tag, but found nothing except a lone cotton ball on the floor beneath it. Lucy took several photos of the chair and was about to send them to her father when something stopped her. The idea that someone had broken into her home, even if just to shock her with an ugly

piece of furniture, somehow seemed more menacing than ants and mysterious cupboard smells.

She concluded that it had to be a practical joke—likely a prank carried out by four mischievous young girls with French braids and too much time on their hands. Making a mental note to keep the house locked at all times, she hauled the chair to the edge of her property, hoping that someone in desperate need of furniture would collect it.

Three days after the arrival of the bunny chair, Lucy had another unexpected visitor: a Siamese cat with large eyes the color of turquoise swimming pools. He appeared on her front porch early one morning during a rainstorm as Lucy collected the newspaper. He happily accepted her chin and ear scratches and just as she was about to return inside, he darted around her legs, through the open door, and disappeared into the darkness of the great house. Hours later, when she took a break from writing, she walked downstairs and discovered her visitor sitting on the very same bunny chair that she'd put to the curb a few days before. Lucy's stomach twisted into a knot. With all the doors and windows locked, there was no logical way that the chair could have made its way back into her living room. Then she heard a soft rattling sound coming from the direction of the chair. The cat was purring. Lucy found herself calmed by the fact that at least someone wasn't unsettled by the chair's reappearance, so she reluctantly decided to leave the chair where it was until she could figure out a better way to dispose of it.

That weekend, Lucy's father arrived to help out with a few house repairs. He brought along a grocery bag filled with New York culinary necessities: bagels, cream cheese, cherry cheesecake, and, most importantly, two pounds of her favorite coffee from a Greenwich Village bakery called Victory to Agnes—an unusual name with a lengthy explanation posted by the cash register that Lucy had always been too impatient to read. He also gave her a tool belt adorned with a yellow bow; Lucy immediately put it on and together they began repairs on the back step. As they worked, Lucy debated telling her father about the break-ins and the bunny chair, but she didn't want to worry him—especially since she'd convinced herself that the culprits were only neighborhood kids.

When the second incident occurred, Lucy and her father had just returned from papering the neighborhood in *Found Cat!* flyers. They walked into the kitchen to discover it waiting for them—a monstrous cake, dark brown, five layers high, with white cream oozing between each layer and topped with a ring of candied cherries shellacked in a thick red syrup.

"It's gruesome," her father remarked.

Lucy nodded in agreement. Never had she seen a cake that looked so entirely unappetizing. For a while they studied it, their heads tilting in unison from side to side, taking in every angle, half expecting it to make a sudden movement. But it remained still, except for a slow trickle of syrup that slid down the side of the cake, forming a sticky red puddle on the kitchen table. Eventually, her father took a fork and poked at the cake several times. Lucy did the same, only she took a piece of the cake, sniffed it, and then put it in her mouth. It tasted like nothing.

"It's that good?" Her father laughed as he watched Lucy spit the cake into the sink.

For a moment Lucy debated telling her father the truth—about the cake and the bunny chair—but a lie came out instead.

"I gave my next-door neighbor my key, just in case she needed to borrow a cup of sugar or something. I guess this is her version of a welcome-to-the-neighborhood present."

"Well then, it looks like you might have a friendly neighbor problem—and I hear they're harder to get rid of than mice."

After her dad left early Monday morning, Lucy drank two cups of Victory to Agnes coffee, put on her new tool belt, and set to work on defending the house against the next prank. She had considered asking for more money from her dad to invest in some video surveillance equipment, but she didn't want to arouse any suspicion. Instead, she settled for the least expensive option: she nailed the lower windows shut and set up a string of pots and pans across the back entrance, never giving thought to how she might access the back porch easily. She felt foolish, like a frustrated cartoon character, protecting her property from a pesky intruder, knowing there was a strong likelihood that it would all backfire on her in some comedic way. Just as she was about to figure out what could be done to the front door, she noticed something moving on the porch. Through the frosted-glass window, she could make out the outline of a woman in a red skirt cradling something in her arms. Suddenly, the woman moved forward, pressing her nose and eyelashes against the glass, fogging the window white. Lucy threw the door open, screwdriver in hand, startling the young woman.

"Oh—my! I didn't mean to scare you!" the girl said as she pre-sented Lucy with a large gift basket. "My name is Scarlett Charm and I'm a student at Ladywyck Lodge. We heard that you arrived early, so I wanted to invite you to next month's pottery social at the lodge."

Scarlett was about Lucy's age, with golden skin, large hazel eyes, and a spray of coffee-colored freckles across the bridge of her nose and cheeks.

"I hear you're going to be one of the flower girls," she said while digging into her purse. She removed a yellow envelope and handed it to Lucy.

"Flower girls?"

"It's our nickname for the students in the floral artistry program. Well, unless you're a guy—then you're a flower boy—which never really goes down well. Our programs sometimes intermingle a little. I'm majoring in herbalism and botany. Go ahead, open it!" Scarlett said, looking at the envelope in Lucy's hand.

Lucy tore the envelope open and a flurry of pink-and-yellow flowers sprinkled to her feet.

"It's purslane. I know some people think it's a weed, but it's really not. Did you know it can ward off evil? Sage is pretty trendy right now, but if you ask me, purslane is much more effective."

Lucy had never heard of purslane before, or its superpowers.

"Don't pick up the flowers. Leave them on the porch—you know—for protection," Scarlett insisted.

Lucy unfolded the invite to the pottery social and immediately recalled the mermaid mug she had crafted in her eighth-grade art

class. It was so poorly made that it blew up in the kiln, taking out eight of her fellow classmates' mugs as well.

"Oh, I'm actually not much of a crafter, especially when it comes to pottery."

Scarlett laughed. "Don't worry, you won't be making any pottery. It's actually just a social—an excuse to gossip and eat cake. We hold the event in the pottery studio, which is how it got its name. Do you bake?"

"Not really. Unless it comes in a box with instructions, then I'm usually okay—why?"

"The social is actually potluck, and the Ladywyck crowd really loves their sweets, so if you do bring something, I would recommend a dessert. I'm bringing my great-grandmother's cinnamon buns. They're always a hit."

Lucy took Scarlett on a quick tour of the house and gardens, hoping that the young woman might be able to recommend it to other students in need of accommodation for the upcoming school year. They talked about the town's best bookstores, tearooms, and thrift shops, but mostly Scarlett liked to talk about Ladywyck.

"I didn't realize that the lodge had degree programs," Lucy said as they headed into the back garden. "I thought it was more of an arts college."

"That's because the lodge is different things to different people," Scarlett explained. "It's like it knows you and knows what you need."

Lucy didn't know how to respond to such a fantastical statement, and before she had a chance, Scarlett pointed out an invasive weed that was taking over one of the garden beds and insisted that they get rid of it immediately. From there, Scarlett went on a weeding rampage that ended with a substantial swath of Lucy's garden in the compost pile.

Once Scarlett was satisfied that Lucy's garden was free of all meddlesome plant varieties she went on her way, and Lucy brought the gift basket into the living room and spread the contents across the coffee table. There was a glorious bouquet of wildflowers, a jar of orange-blossom honey, a box of pastel-colored macaroons, and a bag full of shells with a note attached instructing her to spread the shells around her house, preferably near windows and doors, to promote well-being. There was also a bottle of something pink with a label that read *Eugenia's Fairy Water*, and a beeswax candle in a pretty silver cup that smelled a little like horsehair. There were also a dozen business cards from local businesses, including one that stood out from the rest. It was bright, shimmering green with pink lettering:

Emerald Parker

Good Witch Services

Puzzled, Lucy flipped the card over. There was only a phone number printed in pink. Assuming it was a cute name for a cleaning service, Lucy tossed it into her junk drawer along with the other business cards and went in search of a vase for the wildflowers. She found one that was chipped, a near casualty from the move, and carefully arranged the bouquet. Lucy continued into the dining room, stubbing her toe on an old trunk that she had used to transport dishes to her new home, and was about to place the flowers on the fireplace mantel when she came face to face with him. His expression was the same—jolly but slightly sinister, like an evil Santa Claus—and he appeared quite content to be back in his rightful place. Lucy let the vase slip from her fingers, and felt a rush of cold water seep into her sandals.

CHAPTER FOUR

Ghosts

Captain Quill had made the journey from the attic to the dining room without disturbing so much as the dust along the fireplace mantel. His reappearance, seemingly out of thin air, troubled Lucy, but once the shock wore off, she found herself less frightened and more curious about what was becoming her new reality. She took off her wet sandals, mopped up the water, and then returned the flowers to the vase, setting it on the mantel.

As she looked around for her grandmother's mirror, the one that had been hanging above the fireplace prior to Captain Quill's unexpected return, she heard shouting and laughter. It sounded close, so she followed the trail of voices to the living room. From the window, she spotted the French Braids at the edge of her property—three of them piggybacked one on top of another, the fourth one standing at a safe distance, arms crossed, looking up into the trees. Lucy's trees. The girl at the bottom swayed from side to side, buckling under the weight, and just as she began to fall over, the top girl extended her arm and tore something from a tree branch. As she waved it around like a trophy, Lucy was able to see that it was an old rag doll with messy black-yarn hair and a tattered purple dress. The girls hollered with delight at their rescue and then collapsed, their arms and legs splayed across the lawn; they looked like rag dolls themselves. The fourth sister continued to stand alone, observing her sisters with a coolness that made Lucy think she was in charge.

Lucy moved closer to the window, hoping that one of them might notice her. Within a few seconds, she caught the eye of the leader. She was a little older than Lucy had initially thought—possibly fifteen or sixteen—with a pretty face, but her straight eyebrows gave her a serious, more mature look. Lucy smiled, but the girl just watched her with an expression of mild curiosity that reminded Lucy of the way monkeys observed crowds of onlookers at the zoo: a subtle recognition by a similar but separate species. Uncomfortable with their silent exchange, Lucy waved, watching as the girl lifted her hand up as if to return the gesture only to stop, resting her fingers against her lips and exposing long red nails—womanly nails—a stark contrast to her teenage uniform of jean shorts, striped T-shirt, and canvas running shoes. Then her eyes lowered, dismissing Lucy as she bent down, picked up the rag doll, and pressed it against her chest like a child claiming ownership over a favorite toy. She walked away, leaving her sisters lying in the grass.

In an effort to act like a polite neighbor, Lucy decided to introduce herself to the remaining sisters, but by the time she reached the tree, they had vanished. Lucy turned her attention toward the tall maple and noticed a small piece of purple fabric clinging to a branch. Looking farther up, she noticed that several of the tree's limbs

brushed against the side of her house, just beneath an attic window. From her vantage point, it looked as if the window was slightly ajar. She looked back at the tree again and realized how perfectly suited it was for climbing. Considering the surprising gymnastic prowess of the young girls, it wouldn't be difficult for them to scale the tree to her attic window. Lucy walked to her backyard in search of more clues and observed Brenda and her daughter, Marigold, in their backyard. Brenda was seated at a picnic table with a sewing basket, and Marigold had toddled off to the far end of the yard.

"Only as far as the rabbit hutch!" Brenda shouted to Marigold.

Brenda turned and spotted Lucy.

"Lovely day!" Brenda called out.

"Yes, it is!" Lucy shouted in agreement, although she had hardly taken notice of what kind of day it was.

Brenda motioned for her to come over, and Lucy walked in her bare feet across the warm grass and sat down at the picnic table opposite Brenda.

"Was that you shouting earlier?" Brenda asked.

"No, I don't think so." Lucy tried to remember if she had screamed when she saw the portrait of Captain Quill.

"You don't think so?" Brenda laughed.

Lucy rubbed her forehead, as if the gesture would help clear the fog that had begun to settle in her brain. She realized Brenda was talking about the French Braids.

"Those sisters on the opposite side of me were outside my house trying to get something out of my tree, and they were being pretty noisy about it."

"Oh, I see." Brenda opened her sewing basket and went in search of something. "You seem a little far away, is everything okay?"

Lucy hesitated, wondering if she should reveal her suspicions to this woman she hardly knew.

"There have been some unusual things going on in my house," Lucy explained, deciding vagueness was best.

"Ah, the ghost of Captain Quill. Is he up to his old tricks again?"

Lucy paused. "You know?"

"Of course!" Brenda laughed. "Everybody has heard the stories. I don't know if you know this, but he was my great-great-great-uncle." She hesitated, as if counting to make sure she had the right number of *greats*.

Brenda explained that her house had been his workshop, but in his later years, he converted it into a cottage and lived there instead of the main house. The two homes remained in her family until the mid-1970s, when her grandparents had to sell the main house because they couldn't afford the upkeep. They had tried renting it out for a while but found it was too much work. Brenda talked about property lines, taxes, and something about an eviction, but all Lucy could focus on was how odd it was that she had never noticed the similarities between her house and Brenda's cottage before.

"Have you ever experienced anything unusual in your place?" Lucy asked tentatively.

"Like moving furniture and strange voices?" Brenda smiled coyly, watching for Lucy's reaction. "No, nothing strange. But if you were a ghost, wouldn't you rather haunt a great big house like yours than a little place like mine?"

Lucy noted a slight bitterness in Brenda's voice.

"The thing is, I don't believe in ghosts or anything supernatural," Lucy said as she watched Brenda intently thread a needle. "Actually, what do you know about those sisters next door?"

"The Drummond girls? Not too much. They keep to themselves mostly. Their parents are professors in the city, and there's an awful lot of commuting back and forth." Brenda's tone implied a disapproval of their parenting skills. Lucy remembered the term *latchkey kids* from her youth and wondered if the lack of supervision would account for the girls' mischievous behavior. "But I will tell you this—their names are frightful." Brenda's voice lowered, as if speaking the names aloud might summon the girls. "The oldest is Midgely. Then there are the twins, Bertle and Rutha. And the youngest is just called Freck."

A worried look suddenly washed over Brenda's face. Her back stiffened and her eyes widened, glancing sharply over Lucy's shoulder in the direction of her daughter. It was as if some sort of maternal alarm bell had just sounded that only Brenda could hear. She leapt to her feet, hands on hips, and hollered at Marigold to get out of the rabbit hutch immediately, as she was going to soil her new dress. Then she sat down and turned her attention back to her sewing, stabbing the needle forcefully through the cotton as she attached a button. Lucy figured that Brenda was only a few years older than she was, and yet she seemed much older. She had responsibilities and worried about things like grass stains. She probably made grocery lists and monthly budgets, and concerned herself with the proper daily intake of fruits and vegetables. Lucy didn't think she had eaten a leafy green since she'd moved to Esther Wren.

"But aside from their strange names, do you think it's likely that they're behind this? I mean, do you think they're capable of breaking in and moving my furniture around?" Lucy asked.

Brenda looked from side to side and then moved in closer.

"Who knows what they're capable of. Last December, my regular babysitter canceled on me right before my office Christmas party, so in a moment of desperation, I managed to convince Midgely—after offering to pay her double what I normally would—to fill in. When I came home, Marigold was crying in her room, and Midgely was standing in the kitchen wearing an apron, acting like nothing was wrong. The next morning, I kept smelling onions in the kitchen. I opened the oven door and found Marigold's stuffed rabbit, trussed up like a chicken, in a roasting pan on top of a bed of raw carrots, onions, and potatoes. Thank God she didn't turn the oven on! As it was, it took three washes to get the smell of onion out of that rabbit." Brenda sighed. "Next week, for her birthday, Marigold's getting two real rabbits, and to be honest, I'm a little concerned I'll end up with actual rabbit stew."

―――――――――――

That evening after Lucy locked the attic windows, she opened the bottle of Eugenia's Fairy Water from Scarlett's welcome basket and sat down at the dining room table. It tasted more floral and boozy than she had anticipated—like drunken roses. Looking up at Captain Quill's portrait, Lucy decided he no longer appeared menacing, but rather watchful and wise. She felt a sudden camaraderie with him, as if the two of them had weathered a storm together and were a little stronger for it. As Lucy contemplated how she was going to handle the little misfits from next door, she sipped her drink and watched as the sun set and the light in the dining room turned the same deep-red rosy color as the fairy water. It brought to mind a line from that old mariner's poem: "Red sky at night, sailor's delight. Red sky at morning, sailor take warning."

Red sky at night was a good sign. She poured herself another glass and raised it to Captain Quill.

———

Lucy woke the next morning with a feeling that something was terribly wrong. Even before she opened her eyes, she sensed that the room felt heavy and oppressive, as if something had begun to close in on her. Lucy rolled over, and as she opened her eyes, her attention was drawn to an unfamiliar shadow. Following the shadow across the ceiling and down the side of the wall, Lucy tilted her head forward and found herself confronted with the reflection of her own pale face in the mirror of a strange Victorian-style vanity table just opposite her bed. As she stared in confusion at the piece of furniture that had appeared in her bedroom overnight, fear took hold of her in a way that she had never experienced before. Yet in spite of the shock, Lucy had unexpectedly gleaned an understanding of something she had long tried to suppress: the knowledge that her home no longer belonged to her and likely never had.

This new awareness was confirmed as Lucy walked downstairs to find several pieces of her furniture missing, replaced with a ragtag assortment of chairs, tables, and lamps. Lucy was dumbstruck.

Looking up, her stomach turned at the sight of an ornate crystal chandelier hanging, precariously slanted, from the living room ceiling. She looked down to discover that her Persian rug, a treasured flea market find, was missing; in its place was a bright blue rug with frayed edges that from a distance looked as if it was made from terry cloth. But what Lucy found truly chilling were the curtains: thin, white-cotton fabric patterned with bunnies and bunches of carrots hung from every window.

Lucy made her way to the kitchen where she discovered a platter of meat pies, freshly baked and garnished with a single sprig of parsley, cooling on the table. She hesitatingly poked one with her finger and watched as the golden crust flaked and fell onto the plate. Gently she lifted the pie up to her nose. Like the cake that had appeared during her father's visit, the pie smelled of nothing, though it did leave a greasy residue behind on her fingers. While she wiped her hands on a dish towel, Lucy noticed that the light had faded and the room had darkened, as if it were dusk. Lightning flashed and thunder rumbled off in the distance. A damp breeze blew through the room. Lucy  rubbed her arms and looked around for the draft. That was when she saw that her kitchen window had been wrenched open; the nails were torn and ragged, jutting out of the splintered wood. She ran into the dining room and pulled the curtains open to discover the windows, every one, wrenched open. Broken shards of glass and nails lay on the windowsills.

Lucy's heart was pounding so heavily that she thought she could actually hear it. Gradually, she realized the rhythmic pounding was not her heart but something else. At first it was distant, but as it grew closer, she could make out the distinct click-clacking of high heels moving quickly in and out of the upstairs rooms, and then down the second-floor hallway. She reached for a fireplace poker and held it close to her body, using both hands to steady it. Lightning flashed again and thunder rolled overhead. The footsteps stopped suddenly, as if startled by the approaching storm. Rain began to fall in sheets, and the wind blew it through the open window, soaking the curtains and the floor. The footsteps started up again, stomping down the stairs to the front foyer, pausing momentarily before moving into the living room where they were muffled by the new blue rug.

Tension gripped Lucy so tightly that she didn't dare move, not even to blink or breathe. She just listened and watched, readying herself to swing at anything that moved. The release came in the sound of footsteps on the wood floor directly behind her. Lucy pivoted and swung the poker, falling forward to the floor as her weapon cut through thin air. The footsteps continued on, oblivious to the attack, and went into the kitchen. Lucy watched in disbelief as the kitchen light turned on, casting a dim, warm glow against the dining room wall. In the yellow light, Lucy saw the shadow of a figure move about her kitchen, opening drawers and cupboards. Then the light turned off and the invisible footsteps walked back into the dining room, past Lucy, and up the stairs. Lightning struck, followed by a great boom off in the distance. The lights flickered

and went out, and then flickered on again. A succession of electrical whirls and beeps followed as clocks and appliances reset themselves throughout the house. Outside, sirens wailed. Gathering her courage, Lucy climbed to her feet and ran up the stairs in pursuit of the invisible figure. As she rounded the second-floor landing, lightning struck nearby, charging the air with electricity. That was when Lucy saw it, only for a moment: the slender, curved heel of a woman's red shoe. Then, as quickly as it had appeared, it was gone, disappearing up the stairs and out of sight.

CHAPTER FIVE

Spells

Lucy had always liked morning storms, especially if the day's forecast was to be pleasant. Sunlight on wet streets gave the world an iridescent, almost cinematic quality, suggesting that the day ahead would somehow be more exceptional than any other. That morning, however, the rain tapered off, leaving a heavy cloud that threatened another downpour. Lucy wandered from room to room in a trance, her skin sticky with perspiration and her hair a damp, tangled mess. She checked in closets, behind doors, and beneath beds for any sign of the woman with the red shoe, but found nothing—she had vanished into thin air at precisely the same time the rain ended.

Lucy made her way back to the kitchen where she found herself staring at the handwritten directory of important telephone numbers the previous owners had left attached to the fridge door with two plastic fruit magnets. With a shaky hand, she dialed the police station number and waited. Busy. She hung up, waited a few seconds, and dialed again. It rang several times, and then a voice at the other end of the line asked her to hold. She held for several minutes before the voice returned and asked her if it was an emergency. The man on the other end sounded serious and impatient, and Lucy suddenly felt silly. How would she explain that she was being terrorized by an invisible force intent on filling her house with ugly furnishings and unsavory-looking food? Lucy stammered, and reluctantly told him that it wasn't exactly an emergency. He seemed relieved. Most of the power was out in the downtown core, he explained, and a tree had been struck by lightning, which resulted in a fire in the park. Lucy told him that she would call back later.

Out of the corner of her eye, Lucy saw the plate of grease-slicked meat pies and cringed. Before she could think much about it, she opened her junk drawer, searched around for the card, picked up the phone, and dialed the number. She was expecting it to go straight to voice mail, but when she heard the familiar deep voice growl out the words "Millicent Brown of Brown Realty speaking," she almost hung up.

"Millicent?" Lucy asked.

"Yes, that is what I said. Who is this?"

"It's Lucy Crisp."

"Oh."

"Millicent, I would like to speak with you in person, if at all possible."

"What is this about?" Millicent asked sharply.

"It's about the house," Lucy replied. "There's a problem."

"What sort of problem?"

Lucy drew in a deep breath. "I think something is wrong with the house." She bit down on her lip and regretted the words as soon as she spoke them.

There was a moment of silence before Millicent let out an irritated sigh. She told Lucy that the power was out at her office downtown, so Lucy was to come to her house at three o'clock, as she would be working from home the entire day. Lucy agreed, and Millicent hung up the phone without saying good-bye.

Later that day, Lucy dusted off the old bike that the previous owners had left resting against the side of the greenhouse. It was half rust and half red paint, with squeaky brakes, but it served its purpose well enough. Along the way to Millicent's, the sun came out, warming Lucy's back as she rode through the center of town, taking great care to dodge puddles and fallen tree branches. She peddled past the park and saw a team of firefighters standing around a smoldering tree, split down the middle and caked in ash.

Millicent lived in the last house on Lake Lane. It was a desirable address, as all the homes were situated on large private properties that faced toward the lake. Millicent's house was fashioned in an old Federal style, officious in appearance like a historic government building, with the longest driveway and the most front steps Lucy had ever seen. Unsure of what route to take, Lucy rested her bike on the lawn and decided to formally approach the house from the front steps. As she reached the last step, the door suddenly opened, and a dour-looking maid with sloped shoulders greeted her solemnly and invited her in. She instructed Lucy to remove her

sandals, and then gave a disapproving look when Lucy walked onto the freshly vacuumed carpet in her bare feet. The maid hurried her through the imposing foyer to a long corridor and into a small room at the front of the house. The room was pink, and all the accents, from the drapes to the carpet and lampshades, were crimson red.

"It's called Lady Carnation Pink," the maid announced snidely before letting her know that Ms. Brown would be with her shortly. She scurried away, leaving Lucy standing alone and barefoot in the pink room.

Lucy felt conspicuous, but it didn't prevent her from taking a good look around. Although the room was snug, it felt spacious due to the large bay window that revealed a breathtaking view of the rolling green lawn, the lake, and a generous portion of the town. There was a white-marble fireplace at one end with an oil painting of a woman hanging above it, and at the other, an ornate desk intricately carved and embellished with gold trim. Behind the desk was a matching credenza overflowing with Millicent's awards and accolades. Amongst the plaques and important-looking certificates was a clutter of memorabilia and knickknacks, alongside several red tapered candles, and a bouquet of roses in shades of vermilion and amethyst, their rich, velvety petals edging on decay. The display appeared sacred, like an altar, beckoning anyone who stood before it to kneel down and pay homage to Millicent.

Instead, Lucy sat down on a squeaky leather chair and prayed she wouldn't perspire on it. There was something about being inside Millicent's home that made Lucy uncomfortable, as if she had stumbled into a lioness's den right before the dinner hour.

Adding to her discomfort was the feeling that she was being watched. Lucy turned and met the gazes of the woman in the oil painting and her feline companion—draped around her shoulders—smoke-white with penetrating peridot-hued eyes. The woman was beautiful, but she seemed formidable and vaguely familiar to Lucy. She wore a fitted emerald dress with a black mink wrap, and her hair was arranged in a style that suggested the portrait was at least fifty years old. But what captivated Lucy was her hand. It rested on her upper thigh, exaggeratedly long and slender, with nails lacquered in a color that matched Millicent's lampshades. In spite of its feminine perfection, the hand also possessed a cool and sinister

strength—as if it could suddenly come to life and strangle Lucy where she sat.

Lucy turned her back on the portrait and tried her best to ignore it. While she waited, she thought back to that wintry day when she and her father had first met Millicent. On their way to view the house, Millicent had taken them on a circuitous route through the town's more desirable neighborhoods in her great white Cadillac, while she steered haphazardly with her right hand and dangled her cigarette out of the window with her left, leaving a trail of smoke and ash swirling behind them. She had a tendency to stop abruptly when she spotted a house worthy of discussion, offering opinions on the current upkeep. Lucy noticed that she favored two words—*exquisite* and *hideous*—and used them almost interchangeably. Millicent had a difficult time remembering Lucy's name and had taken to calling her Lisa, Laura, and, inexplicably, Sylvia. When Lucy attempted to correct her, Millicent didn't bother to apologize; she just stared blankly, as if she hadn't heard her or couldn't understand why it should matter.

Lucy's flashback was interrupted by a pungent and flowery odor. Millicent's perfume entered the room before she did, an overripe bouquet of lemon, iris, and gardenia, high-pitched and screeching with top notes. Millicent followed and greeted Lucy with the formality of a politician but with none of the facade. The maid trailed in behind Millicent with her head lowered and presented them with a sparse offering of what appeared to be homemade sugar cookies and hot tea. Lucy politely took a cookie and bit down carefully in hopes of preventing any crumbs from falling. The cookie tasted old, and so she avoided the tea.

There was a moment of awkward silence, which prompted Lucy to make an attempt at small talk. She complimented the grandeur of Millicent's house and remarked on the many steps leading up to it.

"I like to see who's coming," Millicent replied matter-of-factly.

Lucy noted the gold binoculars sitting at the end of the desk.

"Now, what exactly is wrong with the house?" Millicent asked, cutting to the point.

After struggling to get the last traces of the dry cookie down, Lucy calmly explained, in chronological order, the series of strange events that had taken place over the past few weeks. Millicent listened, her face masklike and unreadable. When Lucy was done, Millicent opened her desk drawer and took out a jade-plated cigarette case. She lit a cigarette and inhaled deeply.

"Miss Crisp," Millicent said, overemphasizing the sharpness of Lucy's last name. "As compelling as your story is, I don't understand what this has to do with me. Does your father want out of the house sale? Because I can assure you that is no longer an option. Legally—"

Lucy interrupted. "No, we love the house. I just don't know if I can live in it."

"Well, that isn't my problem now, is it? I sold your father a good solid house, and if you have some sort of pest or prankster, it isn't my concern. I suggest this might be more of a matter for the police."

"I suppose you're right," Lucy said, feeling a momentary flash of anger. "My neighbor told me everyone in town knows that my house is haunted. The fact that you failed to disclose that one piece of vital information might be enough to constitute real estate fraud."

Millicent leaned back in her chair and stared at Lucy while appearing to contemplate her limp threat. But then her stare became beady and bloodshot. Lucy nervously shifted in her chair, causing it to release a loud squeaking sound that broke Millicent's focus. She placed her burning cigarette on the edge of an ashtray and walked over to a wood-paneled filing cabinet, and returned with a thick file, slapping it down on the desk. She put on a pair of reading glasses and flipped through the file as Lucy watched, hypnotized by the sight of Millicent's long red nails scratching the corners of each page she turned. Lucy was struck with a disorienting feeling akin to déjà vu. It took her a second to realize that the feeling was caused by Millicent's hand, the same hand that belonged to the woman in the painting. Millicent's hands looked older now, marred with liver spots and tobacco stains, but the elongated fingers were unmistakable.

"Miss Crisp, this is a copy of the file I have kept on your house. I have sold your house several times over, and there is no record of any previous complaints about ghosts."

The thickness of the file worried Lucy.

"How many times have you sold it?" Lucy asked.

"A few times," Millicent said as she eased back in her chair. "To be precise, seventeen, including your sale." She paused while suppressing a cough. "Over twenty-five years, of course."

Alarm bells sounded in Lucy's head. But just as she was about to challenge Millicent, a queasiness set in. The room was getting unusually humid, and the smoky air mixed with all the pink and red decor was making Lucy feel as if she were trapped inside Millicent's mouth.

"You look a little green, Miss Crisp. Are you ill?" Millicent asked, peering at her closely.

Before Lucy could respond, the maid entered the room carrying a glass of water on a silver tray with a starched white napkin and presented it to Lucy. She accepted it, cupping her fingers around the glass and knew, without tasting it, that the water was tepid. For some reason, that made Lucy feel even more nauseated. She set the glass down on a coaster on Millicent's desk and watched as the sunlight hit the glass, revealing tiny flecks of particles floating in it. For a moment, Lucy could have sworn that the particles were alive—squirming and swimming toward the top of the glass. She thought of sea monkeys, the kind that were advertised in the back of comic books when she was young. *Just add water*, she thought.

"Just add water," Lucy whispered aloud. She lifted her head, heavy and aching, and saw Millicent's annoyed face staring back at her.

"Very well, Miss Crisp. I'm glad we cleared that up. Agnes, please show Miss Crisp out." The maid took Lucy by the arm and hurried her to the front door. With two fingers and a raised pinky, she handed Lucy her sandals, and the door slammed shut behind her.

The fresh air helped, but the queasy feeling persisted as Lucy began the long walk to the end of Millicent's property. Her ears buzzed and rang, and her vision darkened and blurred around the edges. On the last step, Lucy grew overwhelmed with nausea, and before she could prepare for it, she threw up the cookie all over the last step. As she regained her composure, she couldn't help but wonder if Millicent had watched it all through gold binoculars.

Lucy went directly to a medical clinic where she was tested for every conceivable toxic substance within the clinic's resources. An elderly doctor was called in to speak to Lucy, which she quickly understood was to evaluate her mental state, given that she'd proclaimed that her realtor had poisoned her with a cookie. He diagnosed her with the stomach flu and prescribed bed rest and plenty of water, followed by a stern lecture about the dangers of an overactive imagination. Lucy tried to protest, but her words turned to liquid on her tongue, so she just nodded and made her way home to her bed, where she remained for almost two days.

Time was measured in a succession of blackouts and fever dreams in which Lucy couldn't discern reality from hallucination. Out of the stillness of the house, Lucy began to sense stirrings. Gradually, the stirrings became more recognizable sounds—the sounds of several people inhabiting her home. Doors opened and closed, dishes clattered on the kitchen table, footsteps from small feet pattered up and down the stairs, and a rambunctious version of "Chopsticks" played on a piano. There were voices as well: children giggling, a man asking for his morning paper, a baby cooing in the room next to her. Lucy even overheard a family sing "Happy Birthday" in an off-tune chorus followed by the honks and rattles of noisemakers.

In the deepest throes of the fever, Lucy experienced a vision. As she lay in her bed, she observed the figures of a young blonde girl with freckles and a red-haired boy walk into her bedroom. The girl gently placed a slice of birthday cake on her bed and then lifted her hand up over Lucy and sprinkled her with rainbow confetti. The boy appeared more reluctant, but eventually he too stepped forward and set down a kazoo and a comic book beside her left arm. The girl put her finger over her lips, warning the boy to be quiet. Then they crept back out of the room, closing the door softly behind them. The vision was so tangible that Lucy could smell the vanilla from the cake, and she could feel with the tip of her finger the metal edge of the kazoo.

When the fever broke a veil was lifted, and reality returned in all its steely clarity. Lucy climbed out of bed and made her way gingerly to the window, using much of her strength to lift up the sash and let in the morning air. She leaned against the window ledge, feeling momentarily reassured by the sight of her neighborhood illuminated in the early-morning light. Lucy wasn't sure if it was the result of her illness, or possibly her disturbing visit with Millicent, but she was certain that what she was experiencing was only the tip of the iceberg. Lucy recalled the dusty glass of water that Millicent's maid had given her and how it made her think of sea monkeys. That memory was bittersweet; it evoked one of the last times in her childhood that she'd been promised magic. But now, for the first time since her comic book–reading years, Lucy was convinced that the world was not all that it presented itself to be.

Exhausted from her brief walk to the window, Lucy was about to return to bed when she heard a screen door slam. The French Braids came tumbling down their back steps and into their backyard. They were excited—on the verge of rowdy—as they ran to the center of the lawn. It was rare to see them with their hair long and loose, dressed in white nightgowns, wild and glowing, like young lady phantoms. Lucy watched as they busied themselves by arranging a

strange display in the grass. In their arms they carried branches and bouquets of wildflowers, a wooden bowl, a hairbrush set on a gold tray, and the old rag doll they had rescued from the tree the other day. The tallest girl, presumably Midgely, lit a tapered blue candle. She picked up the hairbrush, pulled it through her hair several times, and then passed it on to her sister. Each girl took a turn brushing her own hair, and when the brush was returned to Midgely, she examined it, removed the collected hair, and set it in the bowl. Midgely took the candle and lit the hair on fire. Then she gathered her sisters in a circle, clasping hands, and together they turned their faces up to the sky and began to chant.

Lucy moved away from the window and concealed herself in the shadow of the curtain. Clouds gathered overhead, and the rosy morning sky leached to gray. The birds fell silent. Lucy watched the girls' parents walk out onto the back porch dressed in matching white bathrobes. Their mother carried a stack of folded towels while their father sipped from a coffee cup, his eyes fixed firmly on his daughters. A misty rain filled the air, growing heavier as their hushed girlish voices matured into a forceful command. The candle extinguished and smoked. The girls stopped their chanting and bowed their heads—eyes shut tight—as with heaving backs they drew in deep breaths. The youngest was having difficulty staying upright, her head shaking as she groaned. But Lucy's attention was drawn to the rain. It was different than regular rain: soft and silvery, like liquid tinsel. She listened as the raindrops spattered on rooftops, on pavement, and on tree branches. Great big puddles formed in the grass and saturated the hems of the girls' nightgowns. Suddenly the sisters broke from the circle, and the rain immediately lightened to a drizzle. They broke out into boisterous laughter.

"Girls, girls!" their mother called out. "Well done! Far more controlled. You're really improving!"

Their father hurried inside, and then returned with a camera. He instructed them to line up, invoking moans of embarrassment.

"Now come on, ladies. This is an important day! You've finally mastered it. Let's have one for the scrapbook."

The girls clustered together, teeth chattering, shivering in their wet nightgowns, while the youngest raised her face to the sky, stuck out her tongue, and tasted the fruit of her labors.

"Say cheese!" their father yelled, beaming with paternal pride.

"Cheeeeeeeeeese!"

CHAPTER SIX

Witches

1t hadn't occurred to Lucy that summer had begun until she heard the hum of cicadas, their familiar summer song echoing across the treetops like a warning siren. Lucy stopped typing and looked out at her yellow lawn. A heat wave had settled over Esther Wren. It was a lifeless heat, so dry and arid that it had a silencing effect on the town. Unable to work inside her airless house, Lucy had set up a makeshift office in the shadiest spot on her front porch, using the stray pieces of rotting wicker furniture she had found in the greenhouse. But what she gained in the comfort of an occasional breeze she lost with the many distractions that her room with a view provided. Ever since she'd witnessed the French Braids perform their rainmaking ritual, Lucy had become obsessed with the daily activities of her neighbors. She lived in a constant state of suspicion and distrust, and her quizzical eye focused not only on the French Braids, but on the entire street.

She applied a layer of lip balm and watched as the painters returned from their lunch break to the house two doors down from her. With sagging shoulders, they shuffled cans of paint from the van toward the house. It was board-and-batten, stripped gray, and forlorn looking— a storybook haunted house. Lucy watched as one of the painters lay a straight line of white paint along the clapboard, instantly disguising what it once was. She couldn't help but wonder: What darkness were they covering up with fresh coats of alabaster-white paint? Much the same could be said about the entire town, Lucy suspected. Earlier that morning, the bird lady who lived in the pretty Dutch Colonial on the corner erected a fourth birdfeeder on her front lawn. It was a three-storied birdhouse with a red door. A red door. Possibly a Satanic symbol, Lucy imagined. Even Mr. Holland, the elderly widower across the street who cut his lawn every week wearing only a blue bathing suit and loafers, wasn't spared Lucy's scrutiny. As she peered over the top of her sunglasses toward his freshly clipped boxwood hedges, she could only imagine what kind of domestic devilry he got up to, all alone, in his tidy brown bungalow every night.

But if there was one thing Lucy knew for certain, it was that there was a link between her household disturbances and the French Braids' homemade rainstorms. It couldn't be a coincidence that during the recent dry spell, not a single table, rug, or even so much as a coffee cup had magically appeared in her home. All had been quiet, but Lucy knew that didn't mean it was all over. She had considered telling her father but decided against it, knowing he would insist on visiting more often, or worse, moving in for a while. Lucy had for the first time in her life tasted independence, and liked it, but she didn't know if she could live in a house that was prone to random fits of supernatural redecorating. She had come to realize that her only course of action was to solve the mystery. A good place to start would have been the county courthouse, where she could search the property records for the previous owners of her home. Unfortunately, when Lucy had arrived on the steps of the courthouse, she'd discovered that it was undergoing a renovation; all the property records were unavailable for at least three weeks.

Refusing defeat, Lucy had focused her attention on the house itself, exploring every nook and cranny from root cellar to attic, but her sleuthing turned up only one small find: a narrow wooden box hidden away in a compartment under the stairs. When she'd lifted the lid, Lucy was greeted with a row of black eyes and frowning mustached faces looking back at her. She'd gently removed one of the toy soldiers from the box, and as she'd examined his painted blue and red uniform, a faint recollection surfaced of Millicent Brown mentioning that Captain Quill had made children toys. Although Lucy didn't quite know why, her small discovery had felt significant, as if she'd stumbled upon an important clue.

Lucy had displayed the soldiers on the wicker table right next to her typewriter, where she'd just typed out her third draft of a *Housemate Wanted* flyer she intended to post at Ladywyck. She'd hoped that the soldiers would serve as a reminder to always be on the lookout, to be ready and prepared for anything that might come her way. But now, as she relaxed on the porch, she found their black stares to be judgmental—just one more distraction she didn't need. Lucy collected the soldiers, one by one, and returned them to their wooden box. She put on her sandals and walked across her brittle lawn to Brenda's house. Brenda greeted her, looking disheveled, with a tea towel slung over one shoulder and dark circles under her eyes.

Lucy apologized for the intrusion and handed Brenda the box of soldiers. Brenda looked confused, but when she opened the box, her face brightened.

"Where on earth did you find these?" Brenda asked.

"Under my stairs. I figured they might be your uncle's handiwork."

Brenda picked one out of the box and examined it closely.

"Yes, yes, it certainly is. We have a few things that he made, including a rocking horse that I just adore."

"I was wondering if possibly Marigold might like to have them."

Brenda let out a frustrated sigh. "Doubtful. The only thing she has an interest in these days is Bun-Bun and Clover Rose."

"Bun-Bun?" Lucy was confused.

"They're the rabbits I gave her for her birthday."

Lucy felt bad for forgetting Marigold's birthday.

"Please wish her a happy belated birthday from me. If you don't think she will want them, I can take them back."

"Oh no! Even if she doesn't want them, I'll take them. They're just so special. Oh, that reminds me. I have something I've been meaning to give to you too. It's a book that might be of some help—it was in my grandparents' collection. I'll look for it this afternoon when I get a chance," Brenda said as she opened the box again and smiled admiringly at the soldiers.

Watching Brenda's delight at such a small gesture, Lucy was struck with a pang of guilt. "You know, Brenda, I keep meaning to tell you that I'm happy to do some babysitting sometime. I know that you put in long hours at the bank, and I'm home so much that it wouldn't be any problem."

"Oh, that's so nice of you to offer, but I wouldn't want to impose. You're busy with your house, and school will be starting soon." Brenda paused and bit down on her lip. "But I do have a favor I've been meaning to ask you." She removed the tea towel from her shoulder and twisted it anxiously into a knot. "My parents have a cottage up north, in Canada, and every year I take Marigold for a couple of weeks. It's heaven. I can sleep in, read, relax, and let my parents spoil Marigold. The only problem is that it will be a hassle to take the rabbits with us, with the border crossing and all. So, I've been thinking that it's best to leave them here. Would you mind checking in on them? Feeding them? There's really not much to it. Just make sure they have fresh water and plenty of food."

Lucy smiled, nodding her chin up and down repeatedly, hoping it would conceal her reluctance.

Her recent experience with the bunny chair had left Lucy somewhat wary of anything that had long floppy ears and a cottony tail.

As she walked back toward her house, half regretting her neighborly visit, the dry grass crunching beneath her feet like eggshells, she couldn't help but wonder what she was doing in the floral arts program when she couldn't even keep her own grass alive. The time had come to invest in a sprinkler, even if that meant braving old Lyle at Lyle and Sons Hardware.

———————

A blast of icy, fertilizer-scented air greeted Lucy when she entered the hardware store. For a moment she felt dizzy, almost sick from the sudden climate change. While she paused in the doorway to catch her breath, she saw old Lyle in the center aisle, involved in a very intense discussion with a young man about a kitchen tap. Lucy could tell just by the look on his face that it was going to be a long one. Lyle was a talker. Lucy found a yellow sprinkler and headed toward the sales counter, hoping that one of Lyle's less talkative sons would be manning the till. When she passed by the front window, Lucy caught sight of four girls with French braids on the opposite side of the street. They were walking side by side, gang-like, taking over the entire sidewalk and driving all other pedestrians onto the road. She dropped the money on the counter and hurried out the door.

Lucy wasn't entirely sure of what she was doing when she ran out into traffic, clutching her new yellow sprinkler to her chest. It was such a rare event to see the French Braids outside of the confines of their property that she didn't want to miss out on the opportunity to observe them in public. She watched as they made a sudden right turn into Adams Grocery, entering through the exit doors and gracefully leaping over the turnstile, one by one, with their tanned gazelle legs. Lucy clumsily dodged abandoned shopping carts and a display table overflowing with wilting husks of corn until she eventually found her way to the proper entrance. Taped to the glass door was a faded notice:

NO DOGS

NO UNSUPERVISED CHILDREN

NO HELVA JANE

Once inside, she followed the sound of a flip-flop stampede, smacking and skidding along the linoleum floor. Lucy slowed her pace and tried to act natural as she rounded the corner to find the sisters entering the frozen foods section. The youngest, Freck, bolted ahead of the rest, running toward the wall of freezers as if in a race. She yanked open one of the doors and pulled out a carton of ice cream. Midgely caught up to her, tore the carton out of her sister's hands, and put it back in the freezer. She opened another door and removed a box of green Popsicles before heading toward the front of the store with her sisters moping along behind her. Lucy hid behind a display of waffle cones and watched as they paid for the Popsicles. It was a lengthy and awkward process; Midgely picked through her pockets, reluctantly pulling out wrinkled dollar bills, one at a time. The cashier appeared stiff and careful, accepting the money and counting out the change in return, nickel by nickel, all the while not making eye contact with the girl or her sisters.

It occurred to Lucy that there really wasn't anything so unusual about the French Braids' behavior, aside from their preference for lime-flavored Popsicles and apparent frugality. But what was unusual was how other people reacted to them. A hush had fallen over the store as the French Braids had made their way toward the checkout. Customers scurried out of the way as they passed, and parents protectively pulled their children close. The lady behind them in the checkout line stood a good five feet back, nervously clutching her shopping cart as if it were a shield. Yet however much the French Braids were avoided, they were without a doubt the center of attention. Lucy watched as the other shoppers snuck glances from behind product displays and magazine racks, curious, just as she was, as to what the girls might do next.

Back outside, Lucy continued to follow the sisters from a safe distance. They were heading north, in the direction of their home, meandering slowly down old streets that Lucy had never walked before. Mostly the sisters were quiet, seemingly lost in thought, enjoying their bright-green Popsicles. They often stopped to pick flowers, examining them carefully before dropping them to the ground. Lucy followed their flower trail for two blocks as they shifted east, and deeper into unfamiliar neighborhoods. Although Lucy knew she couldn't be very far from home, it felt as if she were worlds away. The atmosphere was fresh and damp. Puddles of water filled the holes in the broken asphalt. Crickets chirped, backyard dogs barked, squirrels tussled up a tree trunk, and a fat snail slid along an old fence post. There was life here, unlike in the rest of the town, which was suffocating silently under the hot sun. The houses were very different as well—smaller than the homes in her neighborhood, and they sat tightly knit on narrow properties, almost touching one another. Most had pointed rooftops, laced with gingerbread trim, and each house was painted in an array of opposing color combinations, ranging from orchid purple and lime to robin's egg blue and dandelion yellow to Lucy's favorite, matte black and pimento red. Victorian Folk. A style she'd always loved.

Lucy had been so mesmerized by her new surroundings that she hadn't even realized she'd lost sight of the French Braids entirely. She paused, holding her breath, and listened for the sound

of their flip-flops, but all she heard were birds chirping and a distant banging sound. She continued to walk, instinctively making a left turn at the first intersection, and headed west until she reached Elizabeth Street, a street name she recognized. Lucy noticed that while the houses grew bigger and retreated farther away from one another, the veil of humidity lifted, the dry heat returned, and the banging sound that she'd heard earlier was growing louder with every step. She slowed and glanced down a narrow driveway. At the end was a dilapidated garden shed overgrown with weeds and flowering vines. An old man holding a broom stood with his back to her. He suddenly reared back and brought the broom down hard against the side of the shed. It shuddered and creaked under the blow.

"Get out, you filth! You devil from hell! Be gone with you!" the old man shouted at the shed.

His posture stiffened, and he turned around to face Lucy, his heavily lined face fixed in a determined scowl. Lucy smiled shyly, uncertain of how to react to the sight of an old man beating up his garden shed. He tipped his straw hat to her then turned back around, lifted the broom, and dealt the shed another firm blow. Lucy continued on her way.

When she returned home, worn and confused from her outing, she saw a brown paper bag sitting on her doorstep. Lucy reached inside and pulled out a thin green paperback book with the title *You Witch!* printed on the front in a plain yellow font. Attached was a sticky note:

Lucy,

This is the book I was telling you about. I'm not sure if it will help much, but chapters six and seven are actually about Esther Wren. You might recognize the author, Clementine Howard, as she wrote that very popular Elle Mort series ten years ago about a teen witch. That was fiction though, and this apparently is not!

    Brenda

PS: I forgot to ask if you wouldn't mind bringing in my mail while we are away? The key to my house is under the pot of geraniums in the backyard. Thanks again for taking care of the rabbits!

Lucy sat down on her porch steps and skimmed through the book. It was old and grimy and smelled like a musty basement. On the back cover was a photograph of a middle-aged woman with a wide toothy grin, alongside a short biography. From what Lucy could gather, Clementine Howard was a British-born feminist author and activist turned "witch theorist" after an unfortunate altercation with a witch in a New York City department store on Boxing Day 1973 that left her with one side of her face paralyzed. She was later cured by a group of witches located in Esther Wren, New York.

"Witches." Lucy mouthed the word quietly to herself. The sound of it felt hollow on her tongue and tight on her lips. An image of a woman with a green face flashed before her eyes. She was dressed in black with a pointy hat. Her hands clutched a straw

Clementine Howard

broom, revealing long fingers and sharp red nails. Millicent's nails. Then the witch's features softened, her green faded, and the black clothes fell to a puddle at her feet. A teenage girl wearing a striped T-shirt, jean shorts, and canvas running shoes was left staring back at her with disinterest. A heavy feeling grew in Lucy's stomach. She had known it for some time, possibly even before she watched the girls summon up the rainstorm in their backyard. But knowing it and believing it were somehow two very different things.

And just as Lucy was coming to terms with the fact that she was living next door to a coven of sister witches, they appeared. In single file, the sisters crossed the street—their bodies lethargic and their skin pink from too much sun. The youngest, who had not yet shed all her baby fat, dragged behind them, scraping her flip-flops against the pavement, barely lifting her feet as she walked. When they passed Lucy's driveway, Midgely turned and met Lucy's gaze. At first her look was blank, but then it sharpened, her lips forming a deliberate smirk as her eyes fixated on Lucy's hands. Lucy looked down to see that she was still holding Clementine's book with the cover facing out. Immediately, she dropped the book to her lap, burying it deep in the fabric of her dress. Midgely's look of amusement waned, and she turned away. Lucy sat frozen, listening to the sound of flip-flops as the girls shuffled up their front porch steps, and waited for the creak of their screen door that typically followed, but heard nothing. Out of the corner of her eye, she could see them lingering on their porch examining the canning jars. Lucy discreetly slipped behind her wilting hydrangea vine and watched them through the holes in the lattice.

There were nine jars lined up along their porch railing, and each jar was silently inspected until the girls reached the last one. It was much darker than the rest, and something about the jar sparked a shared concern over its contents. Midgely held it up to the sun and gave it a good shake while the twins loudly protested. One of the twins attempted to stop her, grabbing her by the shoulder, trying to force her arm down, when a loud sound cut through the air, like ice cracking on a lake. Lucy watched dumbstruck as the jar exploded, spraying the French Braids in fine shards of sparkling glass. A moment of silence followed as the girls stood stunned. Then, the youngest let out a scream—shrill and girlish, echoing across the lawn—that brought the others to join in. Soon their screams evolved into laughter as they chased each other inside, slamming the screen door behind them. An inky vapor hovered in the spot where they had been standing before it gradually dissolved into nothing.

Lucy bolted inside and up the stairs to find her laptop. She typed "Clementine Howard" into the search bar, and after sifting through countless fan sites devoted to the author's teen witch literature, and many more that focused on the strange events surrounding her untimely death, she found several articles that focused on Howard's theories about witches. Lucy was confounded. How had something like this not attracted more attention?

Her answer was found in a video of Clementine Howard promoting *Witch Face?*—her second book—on a daytime talk show in the mid-90s. In an olive-green tweed pantsuit, Howard spoke with the kind of gentle authority that was instantly persuasive. The explanation she gave was simply that witches hid in plain sight. After the decline of mysticism and the rise of science in the nineteenth century, Howard elaborated, witches really didn't need to conceal their true natures; society did it for them. Howard asserted that for every believer there are thousands of non-believers who will go to almost any length to dismiss magic for madness. Those who dared voice their suspicions were typically mocked mercilessly for it. Howard added that she was no exception, and briefly described the professional shaming she encountered from colleagues after she published her first book on the subject of witches. She added that witches had a way of making what they wished to be so. If they don't wish to be noticed, then that is how it is. The camera lingered on Howard, catching a momentary glimpse of unease, likely at the thought of what could entail.

The host, either a skeptic or simply wishing to stir up arguments for better ratings, challenged her.

"But you can't expect us to believe these women have magical powers?" he asked, using exaggerated hand gestures.

"Absolutely I can," Howard responded. "And they are not just women. There are male witches as well. Although they are considerably more rare."

"So, they can turn a person into a toad? They can fly on broomsticks?" the host asked sarcastically.

The audience laughed.

Howard cleared her throat. "Not exactly. Mostly they work through spells."

"So they can't turn people into toads?" the host clarified.

"Well, possibly. But you're likely not going to see it happen—*poof!*—right before your eyes. Very few witches are gifted with instant transformative abilities. Most often, magic is invisible to the naked eye. It's about the alteration from the natural to the unnatural. This can take time. The darkest magic draws its strength from time. When executed properly, it is insidious."

To prove her point, Howard ran off a list of unexplained strange events throughout history that she believed were the consequence of witchcraft. The host appeared bored by the history lesson, so Howard brought up the more recent "Daisy-Did-Not-Doll Murders." The reference struck a chord in Lucy as she remembered watching a late night documentary series on the doll murders a few years ago.

In the last segment, Clementine Howard theorized that there were two distinct species of witches, to which she gave the playful monikers "the Goodies" and "the Baddies." Both were equally prevalent in the world, but they were completely separate in origin. The host asked her if bad witches were evil. The question appeared to catch Howard off guard. After hesitating for a few moments, she responded by playfully stating that they weren't necessarily evil, but they could be quite wicked. The audience laughed. Howard pointed out that she disliked stereotypes, but she claimed that bad witches often bore certain traits perceived to be undesirable by societal standards, particularly for women. "The Baddies are often independent and often do not understand certain social bonds like friendship." Although they frequently marry, Howard surmised it is for procreational purposes, sexual fulfillment, and financial gain. "Although companionship and love are not unheard of among the Baddies, it is considerably more rare than among the Goodies. Above all else, the Baddies are desirous of power and fortune, preferring to use their magic for selfish reasons rather than to help others. But," she noted, "there is value in such traits. It makes them hard workers, creative problem solvers, and often very successful."

The host asked if they were dangerous, and Howard looked directly into the camera. "Well, yes, they certainly can be. But they are still bound by laws, just like us."

"But that didn't seem to stop the witches who cursed those dolls now, did it?" the host sneered.

Suddenly a newspaper article flashed on the screen:

The Daisy-Did-Not-Doll was a pull-string talking doll that was manufactured in America between 1989 and 1996. In 1996, a recall was issued because of an alleged choking hazard. However, an investigative journalist later exposed a far more disturbing version of the recall. He claimed that the dolls instructed children to do terrible things to their family and, as a result, there were fifteen cases of attempted assault and two deaths.

"First of all, I believe it was just one witch who cursed the dolls. And it wasn't a random attack, but rather the result of a long-standing grudge."

"A grudge?" the host balked. "Against whom? Innocent families?"

"No," Howard answered. "It is my understanding that it was a trademark dispute. The dolls were designed by two women who had a falling-out, and when their partnership dissolved, the one set out to destroy the livelihood of the other. But let's discuss good witches for a moment, as we haven't touched on that yet."

Howard went on to explain that good witches prefer more organic pleasures. Their magic is centered on earth elements, and Howard described them as natural humanitarians. Their symbol is oxen, representing "gentle strength in numbers," and they are at their most powerful as a community rather than on their own. Their gifts lie mainly in the arts, and they are particularly talented in culinary arts as well as horticulture.

The host appeared less interested in the good witches, and he went into the audience with his microphone looking for questions. One red-faced and heavyset woman grabbed the microphone and asked Howard if she was a Baddie. Howard assured her that she was not. The woman's face grew redder and her eyes narrowed with skepticism. A young man dressed in military camouflage asked if there had ever been a war between the Goodies and the Baddies. Howard confessed to being asked that question quite often and the answer was no, at least not to her knowledge. If anything, it was more likely for the Baddies to fight amongst themselves. She likened the two species of witches to frogs and fishes all living in the same pond, enjoying the same ecosystem, but instead of pond water, they rely on the same energy. As long as the energy existed, there would be no need to fight. In fact, the more witches in one locale, the better, as it provided a richer and more pure energy source. The host appeared lost at the mention of ecosystem, so Howard altered her analogy. She asked him to imagine a delicious soup cooking up in a big black cauldron. The more ingredients added, the more flavorful the soup, which benefited all witches. And this, she explained, is why they tend to congregate in certain areas where the energy is rich and strong.

One audience member asked if witches use cauldrons to brew up curses; the next asked if they like to use frogs in their spells. Howard looked defeated.

Then the music queued up, and the host stepped into the frame holding Howard's book to the camera. He advised all viewers to pick up their broomsticks and fly to their nearest bookstore to get a copy. He winked.

Lucy shut her laptop. Her mouth was dry and cottony. She felt disoriented, as if she had just woken from a long afternoon nap. She climbed off her bed and went downstairs to get something to drink. As she stood by the sink sipping a glass of water, trying to digest yet another bizarre hour of her life, something niggled at her. Something Clementine Howard had said about animals. Lucy ransacked her desk drawer until she found the acceptance letter from Ladywyck Lodge. She studied the lithograph design on the envelope and realized that what she had mistaken for cows were in fact oxen. The phrase "gentle strength in numbers" repeated through Lucy's head.

CHAPTER SEVEN

Fairies

"Are you just visiting us, or do you live here?" the lady at the tourism office asked Lucy.

"I actually just moved here."

"You did?" The lady picked up a soap from the *Made Locally* display and handed it to her. "Welcome to Esther Wren!"

"Oh, thank you!" Lucy said as she sniffed the soap. The label read *Summer Grasses*, and Lucy was astonished to discover that it smelled exactly like fresh-cut grass.

"I bought the old Quill house—well, actually, my father bought it."

The tourism lady drummed her fingers against the counter as she tried to recall the house, and then her eyes widened.

"My! That's a big old house. How are you making out there? Is it haunted like they say? I've heard that furniture goes missing and then new furniture turns up in its place."

"Yes, I think the ghost must have been a decorator," Lucy joked.

The tourism lady laughed.

"I will be looking for roommates before I start school."

"You're taking classes at the lodge?"

"I'm starting in the fall. Floral artistry."

"Congratulations! You must be very gifted. I hear that they are quite selective with their students. Many apply, and few are chosen. Of course, you know what they say—right? You don't choose Ladywyck; Ladywyck chooses you. It has a very interesting history. Here, read this."

She handed Lucy a leaflet printed entirely in italics:

LADYWYCK LODGE

Perched high on the hill, just opposite the lake from Turner Inn, sits Ladywyck Lodge, one of the most intriguing, mysterious, and architecturally significant buildings of our beautiful town of Esther Wren. Ladywyck Lodge was originally built in England, just outside the village of Bramshott, Hampshire, in the mid-1500s by the prosperous Ladywyck family of London. In 1790, its owner and young heiress, Merry Ladywyck, for reasons unknown, had the lodge painstakingly disassembled and the pieces brought over to the United States by ship. After its disembarkment in New York City, a fleet of oxen, horses, and covered wagons brought the lodge to Esther Wren, a barely formed village at that time. With the help of a skilled architect, Matthew Moore (whom Merry later married), the lodge was reconstructed over a period of five years to an almost exact replica of the original structure.

For more than a century, the lodge remained a private residence for generations of the Ladywyck-Moore family, but during the 1918 influenza pandemic, it was converted into a temporary hospital that surprisingly had the highest recovery rate in the country. In the 1920s, under the supervision of Ladywyck Lodge's heir, Nathan Moore, the lodge was converted into a "private learning residence," acquiring a board of directors and shrouding itself in mystery for many years. Separation and secrecy lead to suspicion, and rumors began to circulate throughout the community as to the lodge's true purpose. Some believed it was a secret university of the occult, while others thought it a hospice or health retreat for the very wealthy. But in the spring of 1969, a lone traveler appeared at the gates of the lodge, followed by another, and another after him. Before long, a steady stream of travelers, hippies, bohemians, and other free spirits descended on the lodge and its many acres. They came from all over: East Coast, West Coast, and even as far as Australia. Their interest in Ladywyck stemmed from the belief that the lodge, the land, and the lake possessed sacred healing powers. They set up camp on the eleven acres and spent their days swimming in the lake and basking in the lodge's perceived mystical energy.

It was a summer of discontent for many of the residents of Esther Wren. Several attempts were made by the town and the police to remove the trespassers. Their free lifestyle and nude bathing in the lake was considered an unwelcome distraction, especially by those residents with lakefront homes. But each

attempt was met with resistance from the directors of
Ladywyck Lodge.

 By the mid-1970s, many of the travelers had moved on,
but a significant number stayed and made the town of Esther
Wren their home. They have raised families, contributed to the
local economy, and have become highly respected members of
our vibrant and eclectic community.

 Presently, Ladywyck Lodge offers a wide range of classes
and lectures to its students and a smaller selection of arts
classes for the rest of the community.

 For more information, please visit:
www.ladywycklodge.com

When Lucy was finished, the tourism lady clasped her hands together and whispered, "I have a confession: I was one of those nude hippie bathers. I really was! Of course, I was thirty pounds lighter." She laughed and patted her belly.

"I'm sure you'll be very happy there. Ladywyck takes excellent care of their students. It's almost as if the lodge knows you and knows exactly what you need." She winked, and Lucy felt the ground shift slightly beneath her feet.

On her way to the Potluck Pottery Social, Lucy placed a tin of brownies that she had distractedly baked the night before into the basket on her bike. The edges were burnt and there was a mild fishy odor to them, likely the result of using the same pan that her father had used to cook up some fresh local perch during his visit. She debated tossing them in the garbage, but she didn't want to arrive empty-handed or, worse, with something store-bought, so she pushed her reservations aside and set off in the direction of Ladywyck Lodge. When she saw the wooden sign for Oxen Walk (appropriately shaped like an ox), Lucy steered her bike onto the narrow gravel lane. The landscape was lush—untouched by the drought that had reduced her own flower gardens to dusty piles of potpourri. Unseen things clucked and croaked at her from the underbrush as she struggled to steer her bike around the rocks and ruts that marred the road. When Lucy reached a wall of spiny-toothed holly, fortress high, she climbed off her bike and walked it through the iron gate. As she looked up, the lodge compelled her to pause. It was spookier and far more imposing than it had appeared earlier, in the winter. The pitch-black timber frames and steep gables cast long and pointed shadows across the front lawn, swallowing the lush gardens in darkness. Lucy removed the basket from her bike and followed the path of snapdragons and foxglove to the front door, which was unusually small and insignificant compared to the rest of the building.

Lucy knocked but there was no response, so she pushed the door open and peeked inside. The entranceway had a low-slung ceiling, but it opened to reveal a two-story foyer with a fireplace and an ornately carved staircase. The scent of wood smoke and wildflowers drew Lucy inside, and she quietly made her way to a table displaying stacks of brochures alongside a bouquet of exotic-looking flowers. Beside the arrangement was a handwritten note card:

This week's arrangement includes the following:
Huckleduck Spurs, Black Lace Ivy, Sour Thyme,
Bloodthorn and Wisp, Tannis Bells,
Feverfew, and Scarlett Charm

As she leaned in a little closer to admire the bouquet, Lucy heard voices coming from a room just off the foyer.

"You can't put Miss Masters next to Lionel Stone!" said a man, sounding exasperated.

"Why not?" a woman inquired.

"He's been giving her the eye lately—if you know what I mean."

The woman sighed. "Lionel gives everyone the eye. Including me after I get my hair done."

"That may be so, but last time I looked, Miss Masters's lips were shut. Now look at them. I think she's flirting with him."

There was a pause.

"Oh—good grief! Ebenezer, you're right! How long has that been going on?" the woman asked.

"Ever since you moved Grace Henderson to the upstairs hallway."

"Well, let's be honest. He never stood a chance with her. But if he keeps this up, we'll have no choice but to hang him in the broom closet."

Lucy poked her head through the door. She spotted Helen standing alone by the far wall in front of a cluster of portrait paintings, holding a feather duster in her hand.

"Excuse me, sorry to bother you," Lucy said softly.

"Oh!" Helen exclaimed. "I didn't hear anyone come in."

Miss Masters

"I'm sorry . . . I didn't mean to intrude," Lucy apologized as she stepped inside the room.

"You're not intruding Lucy—it's wonderful to see you again. I heard you came to town early."

"I did. My dad actually bought a house here, and I've been doing some redecorating over the summer." Lucy glanced around the room to look for the man Helen had just been talking to but saw no one.

"He bought the old Quill house, didn't he?" Helen paused as her eyes expressed unease. "How is it going?"

"Fine!" Lucy said, sounding shriller than intended. She cleared her throat in an attempt to lower her voice an octave.

"Are you sure?" Helen asked skeptically. "That house has a lot of history."

"So I've been discovering. Do you know anything about the house?" Lucy asked.

"Not particularly, but living in this town, you do hear strange rumors. Some say the ghost of Captain Quill haunts it, but I suspect he's fairly harmless. It's quite a big house for just one person, though."

"Yes, it is. I'm looking for a couple of housemates. In fact, I was hoping to post an ad here."

"We have a notice board by the main office. Do you remember where that is?"

Lucy shook her head while Helen hurried over to a desk and returned with a folded piece of paper and a pen. "It's a map of the lodge and the grounds. As you probably remember, the first-floor rooms are open to the public, along with the pottery barn, the boathouse, the gardens, and conservatories. We are doing some renovations to the upstairs classrooms, so a few of our member's-only summer classes are being held on the first floor. Oh, and the tuck shop is off limits to non-members." She put a big X through the tuck shop. "Okay, the main office is here, and right next to it is the notice board. Are you attending the social today?"

Lucy nodded.

"Wonderful! Now, let's see, you are here in the Room of Portraits." She circled it with her pen. "And just directly to your left is where the main office is. When you leave the notice board, turn right and go down the hall and exit through the screen doors. Take the back steps down to the herb garden and you will see a pathway that heads to the Pinery." She drew a long line connecting the two.

"The Pinery?" Lucy asked.

"They're the woods just outside the lodge," Helen explained. "Just follow the footpath, go over a bridge, and you'll see a black barn, which is where the social is. It's a lovely event." Helen handed the map to Lucy.

"Oh, and try to avoid Sweet Alice if you can. She's the swan that lives under the bridge and she's quite prone to nipping."

Lucy thanked Helen and headed out the door.

As she turned the corner, Lucy could have sworn she heard a man's voice mumble, "More like biting."

After she posted her notice, Lucy made her way down the main corridor. It was long and poorly lit with many closed doors—except one. Lucy peeked in and saw that it was a class in session, filled with people of all ages. A tall man with glasses was busy writing what appeared to be mathematical symbols on a chalkboard. He cleared his throat, set the chalk down, and stated with great authority, "More than anything, astral projection is about geography."

The class bowed their heads in unison and began to write.

He continued, "One tends to focus more on the act of leaving one's body, rather than the actual place that the astral body is inhabiting. This space—or rather, this extraordinary terrain—is what we will be discussing today."

He stopped abruptly when he realized he was being watched. Embarrassed, Lucy quickly looked away and hurried down the hall. A few seconds later, the door softly creaked shut.

Near the end of the hall Lucy could hear a woman's voice— melodic with a trace French accent—coming from the conservatory Lucy had been shown earlier in the winter. When Lucy walked past, ,she noticed a small group of people huddled around a table. In the center stood a pretty woman with long hair and chestnut bangs holding up a small plant clipping.

"Lily of the valley is a true woodland seductress," the woman said. "She will entice you with her sweet scent and delicate appearance. But never for a second forget that she is a deceitful temptress. One taste of her could potentially cause heart failure."

Lucy continued toward the set of screen doors at the end of the hall. She exited the lodge and walked down moss-covered steps that squished like sponge cake beneath her sandals. She stopped for a moment to take in the view. From where she stood, she could see clear across the lake to the Turner Inn and its canary-yellow umbrellas. From a distance, Esther Wren looked so small and serene, like a

miniature town in a toy train set. Hardly the kind of place one would expect to be overrun with witches.

Lucy consulted the map again and followed a fern-lined pathway that led into a forest of tall pines. The trail weaved over gnarled roots and around fallen logs, through a patch of lily of the valley (which Lucy nervously hurried past), and then down a slope toward a short wooden bridge. When Lucy reached the bridge, she trod very lightly in hopes of not disturbing the vicious but apparently sweet swan. Once over the bridge, Lucy spotted the black barn nestled at the bottom of a hill facing out onto the lake. Butterflies filled her stomach at the realization that she was about to walk into a room filled with strangers. But when she arrived at the entrance and saw that it was decorated in a garland of wildflowers and myrtle, a warmth flooded over her. And then she heard someone call out her name.

"Lucy! So glad you came!" Scarlett ran to the entrance and hugged her.

"Good to see you!" Lucy replied as she hugged her back. "Did you know that your name is actually the name of a flower? I just read it on the card in the front hall."

"Oh that," Scarlett said dismissively. "They make us do that with our first one."

"First one?"

"Our first creation. I made that flower."

"So, it's like a hybrid?"

"Not exactly. More like from scratch."

"Scratch? Like as in it never existed before?"

"Out of thin air." Scarlett snapped her fingers and laughed.

"You're lucky to have such a pretty name. I dread to think what a Lucy Crisp flower would look like."

"Oh no! It would be lovely. I would imagine it would be similar to Echinacea."

"So, popular with insects but good for the immune system?" Lucy joked.

"No. More like attractive and easygoing, but much tougher than it looks. Echinacea is very resilient."

"I'll take that as a compliment then."

"You should. Come on—I'll introduce you to a few people." She grabbed Lucy's hand and led her into the crowd.

The barn was a charmingly rustic space with whitewashed walls and a wood-plank floor caked in clay dust. Pretty handmade paper lanterns in delicate shades of blue, pink, and green hung from the rafters along with strands of twinkling fairy lights. The crowd was mostly women, and they mingled amongst the potter's wheels and shelves of drying earthenware while sipping their drinks and laughing loudly. One woman stood out from the rest. She was very tall and she wore a flowing blue caftan, and her silver hair was wrapped up like a bird's nest on top of her head. As they approached her, the woman turned her head and flashed her black-mascara-lined eyes on Lucy. Lucy noticed that her skin was covered in a fine layer of gold glitter.

"Eugenia, have you met Lucy yet? She moved into the old Quill house back in May," Scarlett explained.

"Lucy? You're not Lucy," Eugenia stated as she studied her closely. "Lucy scratches my throat like Russian pine needles." Her mouth contorted as if she had just tasted something sour. "You are Lucinda!" She announced it with such dramatic flair that Lucy felt as if she should curtsy or bow or do something other than stand there speechless. Scarlett winked at Lucy and then excused herself. Eugenia grabbed Lucy's hand and placed something in her palm. It was cool and black and shaped like a spade.

"It is iron and it will protect you from them," Eugenia said.

"From who?" Lucy asked.

"The fairies, my dear. They are small but sly and terribly seductive. Watch out for the male fairies—oh! How great their beauty is—such narrow feet! And highly amorous too." She drew in a deep breath and sighed dramatically, swaying from side to side. "But I can tell you have other concerns right now." She steadied herself and fixed her eyes on Lucy.

"Don't worry about your house too much. The answers will come." Eugenia patted her shoulder. "You will figure it all out in good time. In fact, the answer is much closer than you realize." She smiled.

Lucy was shocked that this complete stranger knew about her troubles.

"Do you mean physically close or theoretically close?" Lucy asked excitedly.

Eugenia ignored her. "You know," she added, "there is another one just like yours. It too has such a lovely porch."

"Another house? Where?" Lucy asked.

Eugenia smiled vacantly at Lucy, and then looked up to the ceiling as if she were stargazing. Lucy got the sense that Eugenia was like a radio: she tuned in and out of frequencies quickly.

"Did you enjoy my fairy water?" Eugenia asked, still staring up at the ceiling.

"Oh yes! It was wonderful, kind of like drinking a rose garden. What's in it?"

"Oh, Lucinda, I can't reveal that. It's an old family recipe from the Lord of Bracknell."

"Is he a relative?" Lucy inquired.

"No, my dear." Eugenia laughed. "He is my fairy lover. He kidnapped me for seven days and held me hostage in my back garden last spring."

Her admission was alarming, but before Lucy could figure out an appropriate response, they were interrupted by a stout woman carrying a tray of highball glasses filled with a bubbly golden-green liquid and garnished with sprigs of herbs.

"Would you care for a glass of Siam Queen Tonic?" she asked.

Lucy accepted a glass from the tray.

"It's made from Siam Queen basil. It tastes a little medicinal and a little like black licorice."

Lucy didn't care for medicine or black licorice, but she didn't want to appear rude, so she sipped it cautiously and was relieved to discover that it was actually quite delicious.

The woman smiled. "It's good, isn't it? And it's excellent for the digestion. Which you will be needing later. By the way, I'm Beatrice, but everyone just calls me Bea."

"I'm Lucinda, but everyone just calls me Lucy."

"Nice to meet you, Lucy," Bea said, glancing at Lucy's basket. "Oh, I can see that you brought something. How thoughtful of you!

We never expect that of non-members. Why don't you follow me and set it down with the others." Lucy turned to excuse herself from Eugenia, who was still looking up at the ceiling. As Lucy began to walk away, Eugenia suddenly grabbed her, digging her nails deep into her arm. Her eyes were wide and wild.

"It's the hellcat," Eugenia whispered in a deep and trembling voice. Then her grip loosened and she looked straight ahead vacantly, as if the strange exchange had never happened.

"Don't mind her," Bea said as she led Lucy away. "Eugenia has her good days and her bad days. We like to think of her as . . . well, receptive. Not many like her around these days. But she seems particularly odd lately, though. I think there must be something in the air."

When they reached the refreshment table, Lucy's jaw dropped. Spread out over two long tables was the most lavish display of desserts Lucy had ever seen.

"It really is quite exceptional, isn't it?" Bea exclaimed.

"To say the least," Lucy responded.

"It's mostly desserts, but there are some lovely cheeses and vegetable dishes from our gardens. Many of the desserts are from old family recipes; some go back as many as fifteen generations. Everything is labeled, as you can see. Now, what have you got there?"

"Oh. Just some brownies," Lucy said.

"There's no such thing as 'just some brownies.' Is it a family recipe?"

"Not exactly. I got it off the back of the box," Lucy responded, feeling a little ashamed.

"Well, I'm sure it will be absolutely scrumptious. There's a little spot over there, right beside the 101-year-old date cake, if you care to set it down. We're just about ready, but if you will excuse me for a moment, I must go get some extra cutlery."

Lucy apprehensively lifted the lid on the brownies and caught a whiff of fish and chocolate. Putting her wretched brownies on display would not only be an embarrassment to her, but would also be an insult to all the other desserts on the table, including the really old date cake. She quickly fastened the lid back on the tin and put as much distance as she could between herself and the refreshment table.

She wandered around the room for a while, awkwardly smiling and nodding at unfamiliar faces until she spotted four young girls with French braids clustered in a corner. They were snickering and pointing at a picture on the wall. One of the twins snapped a photo with her phone. Lucy decided that it was time to finally introduce herself.

"Hi! I live next door to you," she said, in her friendliest neighbor voice.

The four girls turned around, and their grins flattened while they looked her up and down.

"I'm Lucy," she said as the sisters continued to study her. "Lucy Crisp."

"I know who you are. I've seen you watching us," Midgely said dryly.

"Oh, I'm sorry. I didn't mean to make you feel uncomfortable. I was just curious."

Their stares deadened, and the twins yawned in unison, as if already bored by the conversation.

"I was actually wondering what you keep in those jars on your porch," Lucy said in an attempt to keep the conversation flowing.

Suddenly, an uncomfortable heat wafted in her direction—like a shared fever had just broken out between the lot of them.

"Why?" Midgely asked.

"No reason, really. I just saw one explode the other day, and I wondered what they contained."

"It's a science experiment. We're in science camp," Midgely stated as the youngest sister belted out a laugh, and then quickly smothered it with her hand.

"Uh, okay. Well, science camp sounds like fun. Do you get to do lots of neat experiments?" Lucy asked, sounding like a clueless grandparent asking her grandchildren about their lives.

"We don't mind it. It gives us something to do," Midgely said unenthusiastically.

"Well, I've never been to science camp, but when I was ten my dad enrolled me in tap dance—"

"There's a ghost in your house," Midgely interrupted.

The girl's bluntness caught Lucy off guard, but she tried to respond as casually as she could.

"I know. It's Captain Quill. He likes to move my furniture around," Lucy said.

"It's not Captain Quill." Midgely rolled her eyes. "She's way worse than that."

Lucy suddenly went from hot to cold.

"She? How do you know it's a she?"

Midgely's lips parted into a grim smile.

"I don't know anything," Midgely said as a veil of boredom fell across her face. "See you around, neighbor."

The sisters walked over to the refreshment table and circled it several times like a pack of hungry wolves. Slowly, they began to pick at the display, beginning with a few cherry tomatoes and carrot sticks before becoming more invasive, pulling the candied cherries off the top of the empire cookies and popping them into their mouths. With every pick and every pull, the room grew more and more airless: nearby conversations silenced, and all eyes fixated on the bad-mannered sisters until Helen appeared. She greeted the girls affectionately, patting Midgely's arm while she spoke, encouraging the girls to help themselves to the buffet. The girls happily obliged, and then walked toward the door with plates heaping with cake. Through the window, Lucy watched as they ran down to the dock, where they sat down and dipped their toes in the water and ate ravenously.

Conversations picked back up as the air returned to the room. Lucy surveyed the wall, looking for the photo that had brought the French Braids to the point of laughter. There were dozens of photographs—candid shots of daily life at the lodge, but most were group photos of members showing off trophies and awards from various bake-offs, craft competitions, and flower shows. Then Lucy caught sight of a vaguely familiar face: Millicent. She stood in the center of a group of six people, holding up a ghastly-looking doll in one hand; in the other hand, she held a small silver trophy in the shape of an apple. Underneath the photo was a tag that read:

First-Place Winner,
Best Apple-Head Doll, 1980.

Lucy bit down on her lip and tried to suppress her own laughter. The realization that Millicent dabbled in crafting apple-head dolls was almost too absurd to bear. But something didn't seem right. The Millicent that Lucy had encountered was not the creative type. She studied the photograph more carefully. It was definitely Millicent, although significantly younger and with more natural-looking hair, but there was something strange about her. The smile. The expression in her eyes did not match her smile. Instead of pride or joy at her win, her eyes revealed something quite different: humiliation.

"You're the one who lives in the haunted mansion, right?" Lucy looked up to see an attractive young man with shoulder-length dark blond hair and day-old scruff standing beside her.

"Well, I wouldn't call it a mansion. It's more of a house. Although, probably a little larger than the average—"

"And is it just you?" He smiled.

"Just me. Except for the ghosts, of course."

The man laughed and extended his hand. "I'm Daniel. Nice to meet you."

"But we call him Old-Fashioned Daniel." Scarlett suddenly appeared at his side.

"Oh, I hate that. Please don't," Daniel said, shaking his head wearily.

"Don't fight it. You love it," Scarlett flirted.

He smiled and looked away. He had an air of lazy privilege about him that was accentuated by his wrinkled linen suit and expensive-looking shoes.

"I bet you're wearing suspenders under that blazer. Aren't you hot?" Scarlett grabbed his lapel and opened his blazer, revealing a pair of cardinal-red suspenders.

"Yes, I am, and no, I'm not." He pulled his blazer closed.

Lucy quickly got the feeling that Scarlett had a crush on Daniel, but she wasn't sure if Daniel felt the same way toward her.

"I saw you earlier. You were speaking to Eugenia." He smirked.

"Yes, she's very interesting," Lucy responded evenly.

"It's funny how being rich allows you the privilege of being *interesting*, rather than crazy." He took a sip of his drink.

"She's rich?" Lucy asked.

"Filthy. Did you know she claims to have been kidnapped by a fairy last April? There were search parties, helicopters, even dogs. As it turns out, she was in a maze in her back garden the whole time, eating rotting berries and drinking dirty pond water. She looked like a muskrat when they finally found her." He laughed.

"Not nice, Daniel." Scarlett waved her finger under his chin, scolding him playfully.

"Oh, go make a plant, Scarlett," he scoffed back. Then he leaned in toward Lucy. "As you can see, I don't exactly fit in around here."

"Well, you do appear to be one of only six men in the room," Lucy responded.

"Trust me, that I don't mind. It's just there's so much . . . *good* in here. It can be stifling." He fluttered his blazer and Lucy caught sight of his red suspenders again.

"You don't have to come, Daniel, if you find us so objectionable," quipped Scarlett. "It is interesting how your classes always seem to end at just the same time that they put the food out."

"Do you study botany too?" Lucy inquired.

Daniel shook his head.

"I teach a couple of courses here."

"Really? What subject?" Lucy asked.

"Oh, this and that," he said as he surveyed the room again.

Lucy figured that with Daniel's laissez-faire attitude, she might be able to get a few honest answers from him as to what Ladywyck Lodge was really all about.

"I think I was given the wrong impression about this place. I thought it was an arts college, but I guess it's a little more than that?"

"You're giving it too much worth. I would consider it more of a day camp for mystics and misfits."

"Come on, Daniel," Scarlett chided him. "We also have botany and horticulture courses, sommelier certification, culinary classes, and in September they will be starting a new theater program. Lady Macbeth—here I come!" Scarlett clapped her hands excitedly.

"Oh, Scarlett, you would make a terrible Lady Macbeth." Daniel laughed, dampening her spirits. "But seriously, sweet Scarlett, I think it's time." He paused and draped his arm casually around Scarlett's shoulders, causing her cheeks to flame pink. "Although, I suspect she already has some idea," he said, looking at Lucy. "Santa is fiction, the Easter Bunny is a ludicrous farce, tooth fairies have long been extinct—well, except in Michigan, according to crazy Eugenia, but witches are—"

The tinkling of a bell interrupted him.

"Welcome, everyone! Welcome!" Lucy turned and saw Bea standing in front of the refreshment tables ringing a small silver bell. She was joined by Helen and two other women with identical long red hair that was parted in the middle and fell to their waists.

"I would like to thank all of you for bringing such a delightful array of tantalizing desserts. I think it's safe to say that you have outdone yourselves this month—especially Wendy and Merry Lane. I can't even conceive how much time went into your marzipan forest—my goodness!" She turned and smiled at the two ladies with the long hair. They blushed and lowered their heads. "I think that just might make the cover of the cookbook this year. Which reminds me, Isadora needs all the recipe entries by next Friday— so all you stragglers out there, get your recipes to her as soon as you can." The woman paused. "Now, I want to take a moment to introduce you to our new guest—Lucy Crisp. Lucy . . . where are you?" Bea said as she teetered on her tippy toes to look amongst the crowd.

Lucy wanted to run and hide. Instead, she felt Daniel's warm hand reach over, grab her arm, and wave it limply in the air.

"Oh, there you are! Lucy, we are so pleased to have you today, and we welcome you to Ladywyck Lodge. For anyone who has not met Lucy yet, she moved into the old Quill house back in May. She comes from New York City and has enrolled in our floral artistry program. We are so delighted to have you join us today."

The crowd applauded as Lucy nodded her head in a mix of appreciation and embarrassment.

"Now then, I don't want to delay any further—we can't have the lovely Spinster Tease melting to a puddle. Everybody please take a plate and enjoy!"

Suddenly, Lucy felt herself caught in a wave of people heading toward the refreshment table, and lost sight of both Scarlett and Daniel. As she got in line and collected her plate and cutlery, a small band began to play and the room filled with music and laughter.

Excited about meeting new people and riding the crest of a sugar high, Lucy left the social and quickly peddled home. Along the way she mulled over her new clues, wondering if there was any merit to them. She was particularly interested in Midgely's statement about her ghost being female, which did make a certain amount of sense, given the red shoe she'd seen on the day of the electrical storm.

When she arrived at her front porch, she was greeted by her cat, whom she had taken to calling Mr. Mews. He had been missing for almost two days. Lucy had noticed that lately he was prone to disappearing for a day, sometimes two, and she was beginning to wonder if he had found another family, one that didn't live in a haunted mansion. Lucy unlocked the door and Mr. Mews ran ahead of her toward the kitchen, meowing his hungry meow. Lucy followed and opened a tin of cat food. As she set it on the floor, she heard the wind suddenly pick up and a branch hit the side of the house, then another. Her body stiffened. Lucy looked toward

the kitchen window, expecting to see a storm approaching; instead, she saw only a stretch of blue sky. She closed her eyes and sighed, letting the tension fall away. When she opened them again, they rested on the mess that was overtaking her kitchen: toast crumbs scattered across the countertop, dirty tea towels bunched into damp balls, and stacks of dishes teetering like towers in the sink. Housework had never been high on Lucy's priority list, and the recent heat wave had made it even less so, but in fear of attracting an ant colony, Lucy slid on a pair of dish gloves and ran the kitchen faucet, filling the sink with soapy bubbles.

Just as Lucy was rinsing the last dish, a dizziness set in. Her ears plugged, and she felt a sensation as if her head had been pushed underwater. Through the open window, she watched the maple trees silently sway like seaweed in a rough current. Lucy drew in several deep breaths and tried to pop her ears, with no success. She leaned against the countertop in an attempt to steady herself, and while she peeled the rubber gloves from her fingers, a feeling of dread washed over her. When Lucy turned around, she saw a man standing in her kitchen doorway.

A scream of shock rang out—short and piercing—startling Lucy, who didn't realize it was her own scream until it had stopped. The man's dark hair was curly and unusually shiny—almost synthetic looking, like a cheap Halloween drugstore wig—and he was dressed in an outdated denim pantsuit, a size too small, with two large pockets crudely stitched onto the front of his jacket. But what disturbed Lucy the most were his eyes. They stared vacantly back at her—wide, unblinking, and lifeless. Then, he took a step forward into the kitchen and stretched out his arms. Lucy noticed that his hands were pale, much paler than his face, and unusually delicate for a man of his size. He turned his head stiffly from side to side as he looked around the room, searching for something.

"It's time for my supper," he announced, his voice a thin echo, and his words not matching the movement of his lips.

The dish gloves slipped from Lucy's hands and hit the floor with a rubbery smack. The sound snapped her out of her shock. She began to move toward the back door, keeping her eyes fixed on the intruder, who was still surveying her kitchen hungrily. When she felt the butcher's twine rub against the back of her legs, it was too late; she was already tumbling backward, taking the string of pots and pans that she had rigged earlier in the spring with her. With hardly any room to fall, Lucy's shoulders took the brunt of the impact, hitting the door with a dull thud, her head narrowly missing the doorknob, and her feet skidding out from beneath her. She landed in a seated position with her legs splayed like a rag doll. Tears welled in her eyes, but she choked them back when she realized the intruder was no longer in the room. In a way, his sudden disappearance bothered her more than his presence—as if he were a watched spider up high in the corner of the room that had vanished overnight and was likely to reappear when least expected.

Lucy climbed to her knees. She was tangled in string, but before she had a chance to free herself, she heard strange noises coming from the dining room. She leaned to the side, careful not to disturb the pots scattered around her, and saw through the open door that the intruder was seated with his back to her at the dining room table.

A feast was laid out before him, with platters of roast turkey and ham, alongside a bread basket, several vegetable dishes, and a pitcher of pink lemonade. In the center of the table was a cake that looked very much like the tasteless Black Forest cake that had appeared in her kitchen earlier in the summer—it too oozed and dripped like a confectionary infection. She listened with disgust to the sound of his wet lips mushing together as he ingested thick mouthfuls of food, grunting with pleasure as he chewed. When she saw his greasy hands reach out and roughly rip a drumstick from the turkey, his presence suddenly felt more threatening. Lucy reached for the doorknob and jiggled the lock until she felt it release. Still trussed up in butcher's twine, she scrambled outside on her hands and knees, dragging the garland of pots and pans behind her.

CHAPTER EIGHT

Help

Lucy waited at the police station in a windowless office for almost an hour with a copper pot on her lap. She had run five blocks, stopping only once at the end of her own street to untie the string that was caught in the buckle on her sandal. One medium-sized saucepot remained attached to the string, and not knowing what to do with it, she carried it with her to the police station.

The door opened, and a police officer walked into the room carrying a pencil and a notepad. His uniform was tight and beads of sweat gathered across his brow. He offered her a cup of coffee, which she gratefully accepted. It tasted bitter and watery, like it had been dispensed from a vending machine.

"Ms. Crisp, I'm Officer Brian Norton. I understand you had an intruder in your home?" he said as he sat down across from her.

"Yes," Lucy responded.

"I see. Well, Ms. Crisp, we sent over two officers to investigate, and the intruder is no longer there."

Lucy let out a sigh that the officer took for relief, when in fact it was actually frustration. She had hoped that someone else would bear witness to what she had been dealing with for the past month and a half.

"Now, I want you to write down on this notepad everything you can remember. I understand that he spoke to you? What did he say?"

"He announced that it was time for his supper," Lucy said as she put the pot on the desk.

The officer's brow furrowed.

"He wanted you to make him dinner?"

"Not exactly. It didn't feel like he was really talking to me. It's hard to explain," Lucy responded.

The officer looked down at the copper pot on the desk. "Is that why you brought a pot with you?"

"Oh—this? No. I tripped on the string of pots and pans at my back door and this one kind of attached itself to my sandal," Lucy explained, knowing she was losing credibility with every word that she spoke.

"I see. And you mentioned to the officer at the front desk that when you left the house, the intruder was seated at your dining room table—eating?"

"Yes, that's right."

"But you also told the officer that it wasn't your food. That it had just appeared?"

"Yes, that's right."

The officer rubbed his forehead. "Can you explain how the food got there? Did he bring it with him? Like a picnic or something?"

"No. I don't think so." Lucy could see by the expression on his face that he was struggling to understand.

"Well, the investigating officers claim that there was no food in your dining room, but there was an empty bottle of illegal alcohol sitting on the dining room table. I believe it's Eugenia Forrester's Fairy Water."

Lucy knew she should have tossed away the empty bottle, but the label was so pretty that she'd decided to keep it, certain it would make a perfect vase for a rose or hydrangea flower. Instead, it just sat on her dining room table collecting dust and the occasional fly.

"I think this was a mistake." Lucy stood up and walked toward the door. "I should never have come here."

"Ms. Crisp—wait a second!"

And just when Lucy thought the officer was about to actually be of some help, she looked over her shoulder to see him waving the copper pot in the air.

"Don't forget your pot!" he shouted.

Lucy left the police station and walked around aimlessly. The streets were almost empty—swept clean by the windstorm of tourists who were huddled safely inside restaurants, peering out at her from behind their bread baskets and glasses of local pinot noir. But the wind was the least of her concerns. She felt alone and tired and confused and she wanted to go home to New York where she could cry on her dad's shoulder. He would console her by whipping up her favorite meal (lemon-basil roasted chicken with mashed potatoes), and the next morning they would sit down and hash out a plan. But she knew this was something that a home-cooked meal and a well-meaning dad couldn't easily fix. She regretted not telling him about the disturbances as soon as they began; now that she was so deep in it, she didn't know where to begin. Lucy looked across the lake and saw the Ladywyck lights reflected on the water. The building felt like a beacon of hope in the growing darkness.

Night had fallen by the time she reached Oxen Walk. There were no streetlights or stars, so Lucy stumbled along blindly, jumping at every rustle and snapping twig, relieved to have the copper pot in hand, especially when a creature—thin and whiskered—skittered past her leg. At some point, she realized that the wind had died down to an unearthly stillness: the loudest sound was that of her own breath and the dry scrape of gravel beneath her feet. As she neared the lodge she saw splinters of light cutting through the bars of the iron gates and was relieved that they were still open, although she hadn't given much thought as to what she was going to do once inside. She figured she would find Helen or Eugenia or some other well-meaning Goodie, share the story of her house troubles, and hopefully get some advice on how to handle her haunting.

Just beyond the gate, a lone figure moved across the lawn. Lucy stood back and watched it pace back and forth several times. There was something about the way the figure moved, with a sort of slouched elegance, that told Lucy not to be afraid.

"Lucy?" A voice resembling Daniel's called out to her.

"It's me." She stepped forward and waved the pot in the air.

"I knew I recognized that braid."

As he approached her, Lucy understood what Scarlett saw in him. He was striking, even more so in the dark with the lights from the lodge illuminating his chiseled chin and cheekbones. Most of the boys Lucy had befriended up until now were just that: boys. Still to be weaned from their video games and skateboards. Daniel was all grown up, likely in his mid-twenties, but he still retained one of the more charming aspects of young men: a steady look of mischief in his coin-gray eyes.

"It's a little late for a cooking class," he announced, observing the pot in her hand. "I'm not sure what culinary school is like in the big city, but here we provide the pots and pans," he teased.

"Hi, Daniel. What are you doing wandering around in the dark?"

"That's just it," he said as he squinted at the night sky. "I'm wandering around in the dark."

"Are you waiting for someone?"

Daniel nodded. "I'm too early though. There's no moon yet. Are there stars? I can't see any."

"No stars. I think it's pretty overcast. Maybe, if we're lucky, we'll get some rain."

"Not likely," he said. "So, what are you doing with a pot? Are you going camping? Are you secretly a Girl Scout?"

Lucy held up the three fingers of her right hand and saluted him. She figured it was easier to play along with his joke than to tell him the real story of how she and the pot became so attached.

"I'm not surprised. You've got the look," he said, eyeing her braid. "And speaking of girl things, I just saw your pretty pink ad on the notice board inside. One complaint though: I don't think it's quite pink enough."

"Yeah, I don't know what I was thinking. I guess I just wanted it noticed."

"Well, noticed or not, there's no way you're going to get a house-mate. Everyone around here knows your place is supernaturally challenged."

"Everyone but me, that is."

"I detect a little self-pity," Daniel said, pouting his lower lip in a mocking manner. "You need a distraction. Have you had a tour of this place yet?"

"Helen showed me the first floor and the gardens when I visited earlier in the winter."

"Ah, so you've had the censored tour. Let me give you the uncensored one. The Goodies are probably all tucked up in their beds right now, so I may be able to show you the things they don't want you to see. During the summer the lodge is pretty much reduced to a skeleton staff and only a couple of guardians."

"What exactly *is* a guardian? I mean, I know that Helen is one, but I don't really understand what she does."

"Join the club. It's all very mysterious, but from what I understand the guardians care for the lodge."

"Like janitors or groundskeepers?"

"Not exactly. It's slightly more complicated than that. You see, some say that the lodge possesses its own magic."

"Like witches?"

"Yeah, I guess you could say that," Daniel replied as he chivalrously opened the front door, gesturing for her to go inside. As she passed by him, she caught his scent—rich and warm—like sandalwood. Her stomach did a somersault. "And that kind of magic has to be guarded and cared for."

"Guarded from what?"

"From those who want to take it. The lodge is valuable, and I'm not just talking about dollars and cents—if you catch my drift."

Lucy thought about Scarlett's cryptic statement about how the lodge knows you and knows what you need, and how the tourism office lady had repeated the same sentiment. Lucy wondered what the lodge knew about her. She instinctively ran her fingertips along the wooden wainscoting and thought she felt it move slightly—like a twitch.

Daniel ushered her down the hallway and stopped in front of the door to the Room of Portraits.

"I like this time of year. It's nice and quiet. Well, except for this bunch." He paused and cocked his ear to the door, motioning for Lucy to do the same. Lucy could hear whispering inside.

Daniel knocked on the door and opened it. The whispers fell silent.

"These guys are usually last to bed. I should first warn you to never say anything in this room that you don't want repeated. Only a couple of them can keep a secret." Daniel walked to the center of the room and pointed up to the far corner. "That's Lionel Stone over there on the far right. Women, particularly, should never make eye contact with him. He's a lusty one and, if you listen to what the others say, a chauvinist pig. Over on the far left is Madame Claire Dubois. She has a bad back and never stops moaning about it. Then there's Mr. and Mrs. Morris; they're a little dull. Miss Masters is all right, and Ebenezer Edwards is a tattletale and likes to boss everyone around. Now, where's Grace Henderson? She's the great beauty of the bunch—that is, if you like that blonde, patrician Princess Grace type."

"They moved her to the upstairs hallway. I think Lionel Stone was sexually harassing her."

"How do you know that? Are you telepathic?"

"Maybe," Lucy said coyly. "But who are these people?" Lucy asked, feeling the weight of their gazes upon her.

"Some say they serve as the eyes and ears of this place. Lionel would say they are the ones who make all the decisions around here, but Lionel has a tendency to inflate his importance. Although Cyril over there—in the green evening gown with the lazy eye—is likely the one in charge. She's quiet, and I suspect still waters run deep. Now, let's leave these talking heads to their evening whispers, and I'll show you something that is completely off limits to non-members."

Lucy followed Daniel to a steep back staircase and watched him remove a lighter from his pocket. In the dim glow of the flickering flame they walked up four flights of stairs, and then down a hall toward a closed door. She was aware that creeping around a house of sleeping witches, alongside one that she suspected was a Baddie, was likely not the wisest decision, but somehow it still felt safer than being inside her own home. Then the flame went out.

"Daniel?" Lucy whispered into the dark.

She heard a door creak open, and then inhaled a waft of stale air that smelled like camphor and old fabric, reminding her of the scent of her grandmother's linen closet. She heard footsteps on wooden floorboards, a dull thud, and then silence.

"Daniel? Where are you?"

Suddenly a lamp turned on.

"Much better." Daniel sighed and rubbed his elbow.

He stood a few feet into an attic space that looked as if a museum had collided with a rummage sale.

"Welcome to the Room of Curiosities!" Daniel announced proudly. "Everything in this room is either enchanted or spellbound. It's all pretty harmless, but don't touch anything, just in case," he said as he picked up a red velvet pouch and waved it in the air.

"What's that?"

"This is the Seven Loves of Abigail Webster Locket."

"And it's enchanted?" Lucy asked, moving in to take a closer look.

"What do you think?" Daniel slid the locket out of the pouch and opened it to reveal a black-and-white photograph of a pretty dark-haired woman on one side and, on the other side, a man with a mustache. He closed it and opened it again. The dark-haired woman was the same, but the other picture had changed, this time to a clean-shaven blond man. Daniel repeated the gesture several times, and every time he opened the locket, a different lover was revealed.

"I think it's safe to say that Abigail has significantly more than just seven loves." He shut the locket and slid it back into its draw-string pouch.

"And over here is one of Scarlett's immortal orchids. Apparently, they will survive forever under any conditions—even without water or sun. They make great hostess gifts. I have two. And over there is a storm jar," he said, pointing to a pitch-black bell jar sitting alone

on a table. "It's an old one—dated 1780, and I think the label says that it comes from the Normandy region of France."

Although the jar was old and quite decorative, something about it reminded Lucy of the canning jars lined up along the French Braids' porch. The sides were dripping with condensation, but as she drew closer she could hear wind howling and rain lashing against the sides. Daniel kept a safe distance from it.

"Whatever you do, don't lift the top off. You'll let it out."

"Let what out?"

"The storm. It's over two hundred years in the making. God knows what that would be like if it was ever unleashed. We have a few more of them, scattered around the room. There's even a monsoon from Thailand in the back corner."

"How did all this stuff get here?"

"Well, not surprisingly, quite a few things have been plucked from local garage sales. But some just arrive in crates and boxes. Sometimes the lodge sends guardians overseas to collect the trickier items that shouldn't be shipped, but most of it just finds its way here." He picked up a toy wooden sword and playfully stabbed it at a suit of armor, gashing the metal.

Lucy walked down one of the pathways, taking it all in while being careful to not disturb anything. She noticed that there was no apparent order to any of the items—piles of cookbooks lay next to yellowing wedding gowns and toy figurines were stacked next to vintage radios. Most items had a label attached, usually neatly typed, that gave some sort of explanation of its history or purpose. Lucy spotted an old children's book without a visible tag and paused. It was likely about fifty years old, and the cracked cover illustration depicted a fluffy sheep dog happily playing with a stick while two children dressed like pilgrims stood in the doorway of a quaint log cabin. The title read *The Tale of the Time-Traveling Dog.*

"I wonder what magic this book holds," she said, pointing toward it.

Daniel, who was now wearing a blue velvet cape embroidered with silver stars, and still holding the toy sword, swooped in to take a look.

"Hmm. I don't think I've ever noticed this before." He picked the book up and flipped through the pages of candy-colored illustrations. "Whatever it is, it looks pretty tame to me." He set it back down and then paused. Then he picked it up again, tipped it upside down and shook it several times. He opened it back up to reveal nothing but blank pages. "Looks like the story fell out!" He laughed while Lucy's eyes frantically searched the floor, not really understanding what she was searching for.

"It's one of the Runaways!" he exclaimed. "The story goes that there was this hippie witch—a Goodie—who got it in his head that stories shouldn't be bound to the pages of books. It was the sixties, so I'm sure he was high or something. Anyway, he went around to a bunch of bookstores and cast spells that released the stories. The media had a feeding frenzy that year. All kinds of crazy things were being reported—aliens, bands of pirates looting museums, dinosaurs wandering the countryside, dead presidents dining in restaurants. The Goodies of course rallied together and cleaned up most of his mess, returning the stories to their pages, but once you've tasted freedom, like the time-traveling dog here, it's hard to stay put. I bet Rover is now running wild a few streets over."

Lucy felt something stirring inside of her, a twinge of inspiration. But it was still intangible—a brilliant idea just beyond her reach.

"And here's something else they don't want you to see." Daniel interrupted Lucy's focus as he reached into his suit pocket and pulled out a small booklet. "It's the Member's Only Course Calendar, and you won't find any finger-puppet workshops here. But there is the popular Séance Etiquette 101." Daniel laughed. "Do you know they teach you how to discreetly throw up ectoplasm in that course? Like there's a polite way to do that. Oh—then there's The Mating Ritual of the Common Garden Fairy—riveting stuff." Daniel shook his head. "There's also Banshees: Messengers of Death or Simply Misunderstood?"

"Banshees?" Lucy said, almost choking on the word.

"Sure. Didn't you know we have them in Esther Wren?"

"Them?"

"Three actually. Well, two are useless. One is really old and has dementia; so if she comes to your window in the middle of the night to warn you about your impending death, don't take it too seriously. The other one is always pregnant and doesn't get very far—mostly she just floats above the gas station on Griffin Avenue."

"And the third?"

"That would be Adelaide. She's something else. I've clocked her speed at a hundred miles per hour." Daniel walked over to a little curio cabinet and pulled out a lock of white hair tied with a red ribbon. There was a little tag attached to the ribbon that read:

BANSHEE HAIR

Found April 17, 2012, in Pitch Pines at the corner of
Eve Street and Lockmore Road, Esther Wren, NY.
Believed to belong to Adelaide Morrigan.

"She's fast, but sometimes clumsy. Trees can be an issue, especially if she accelerates too quickly."

Lucy hovered her index finger overtop of the hair.

"I know I said not to touch anything, but this is safe. Go ahead, it won't bite."

Lucy was surprised that it felt soft and silken, not coarse, as it appeared.

"Do you know her?"

"Not really. She doesn't hang around the lodge, but sometimes I see her at the coffee house on evenings when bands play. Banshees are an interesting bunch. By day they're completely normal people with no magical talents or abilities, but at night, when they fall asleep, they transform. We tend to dislike them—claiming that they're just overgrown fairies—but the Goodies are kind of freaked out by them. You know, because they can foresee a person's death. It doesn't help that when they transform their hair goes white and they wail a lot. But I think Adelaide is most beautiful when she's completely wild and free."

He looked back down at the hair and his eyes softened. He tenderly placed it back in the curio cabinet and, at that moment, Lucy understood that neither she nor Scarlett stood a chance with Daniel. Her crush that had barely gained traction came to a screeching halt.

"So, what course do you teach?" Lucy asked.

Daniel flipped to the middle of the booklet and pointed to Fool's Gold—Charlatans, Tricksters, and Grifter Witches: An Exploration of Their Influence on the Modern-Day Banking Industry.

"Fool's Gold—what's that?"

"Fool's Gold appears like regular money—looks like it, feels like it, and even smells like it—but it disappears after it has exchanged hands. Essentially, it's counterfeiting without the pesky paper trail. My theory is that all those sub-prime mortgage deals, not to mention penny stocks and a good portion of hedge funds, are all just fancier forms of Fool's Gold. Here, take this," Daniel said, digging into his wallet and pulling out a twenty-dollar bill. He handed it to Lucy. "Put it in your purse." Lucy happily took the money and tucked it into her purse.

"Okay, now take it out," Daniel instructed.

Lucy reached back into her purse, but the money was gone.

"Ha! That's so—"

"Daniel." A serious voice rose up from behind them.

Lucy and Daniel turned around to see Helen standing just inside the door.

"Helen—hi!" Daniel said, stuffing the course calendar back into his pocket.

"It's hard to get any sleep with the two of you stomping around like elephants," she said curtly.

"There's no way you can hear us all the way over in the East Wing."

"No, but my room is being redecorated so I've been sleeping in the Acacia Room, which is right underneath your feet." She lightly tapped her foot on the floorboard. Helen's attention focused on Lucy.

"It's nice to see you again, Lucy, but it is almost midnight and I think you should be heading home now." She turned her attention back to Daniel. "And I would like to see you in my office, Daniel, first thing tomorrow."

Daniel nodded and took off the cape. He then picked up Lucy's pot, which received a raised eyebrow from Helen, and they all left the room. Helen escorted them down the steps to the front door and instructed Daniel to make sure Lucy got home safely.

Daniel's vintage European car took three attempts to start. Daniel spoke to it gently—coaxing it into submission until it back-fired and sprang to life. He grinned smugly and patted the dash-board, then floored the gas. As soon as they turned off Oxen Walk and headed toward downtown, the wind picked up again—leaves and twigs pelted against the windshield. Daniel had grown quiet and distant, and Lucy wondered if he was worried about being caught out by Helen. Or possibly he resented having to drive her home? She made a few attempts to continue their earlier conversation—discuss-ing the possible whereabouts of the time-traveling dog—but Daniel seemed to have lost interest and concentrated his efforts on driving his tin-can car at a nausea-inducing speed. By the time they pulled up in front of her house, Lucy felt as if she was sitting next to a com-pletely different person than the one she had played show-and-tell with all evening. She climbed out of the car and thanked him. His response was a churlish "Yup," delivered as he sped away without bothering to see if she had gotten inside safely.

Lucy stood curbside in a puff of diesel fumes and stared toward her house, which was lit up like a birthday cake. Every light blazed

from the windows, giving her home an unexpectedly festive appearance—as if a party was about to begin and she was anticipating guests. Inside, Lucy discovered that the police had been very meticulous. Almost every door to every room and closet was wide open, along with several cupboards. Lucy closed the cupboards and then switched off all the lights except the ones in the living room. She settled into the sofa with a paperback and a fireplace poker for protection. She struggled through the first chapter until her imagination got the better of her—luring her out of the pages of her book and into the blackness of her own front hallway. Lucy pictured the intruder's lifeless eyes materializing out of the dark and shuddered. She returned to the sofa, lay back on the pillow, and tried to think of more pleasant things—like the lusty Lionel Stone and the Seven Loves of Abigail Webster Locket. She thought about the Potluck Pottery Social and the endless dessert display and then tried to recite as many of them in her head as she could recall: *Strawberry Spinster Tease, Vanilla Possets with Lavender Ice Cream, Chocolate Fudge Penny Cake, Baked Apple Eleanors, Mint Maudlin Maudes, 101-Year-Old Date Cake, Peanut Butter Prim and Propers, Lemon Lusts, Withered Sister Tea Cakes, The Big Blonde Bundt Cake, Jammy Jelly Buns, Whipped Raspberry Fool, Flies in the Graveyard, Sea Salt and Black Pepper Pudding, Tippy Tippy Toffee Trifle, Coconut and Cockles Pie, Summer Snowballs, Caramel Crème Tasties, Fairy Teardrops . . .*

After a while, the desserts blurred and blended together, their names drifting further from memory as she was lulled into a shallow sleep.

At daybreak, Lucy woke to the sound of wind. It rattled the window-panes and hissed through every crack in the house. The dining room fireplace groaned, and a heavy dusting of soot showered the hearth. Lucy sat up and opened the bunny drapes to discover that the blustery winds of yesterday had steadily increased into a near hurricane. Tree branches lashed wildly against a yellow-tinged sky, and her wilting garden was ragged—its leaves and flowers strewn across neighboring lawns and driveways. Mr. Mews walked into the room and paused. His ears pricked up and his tail bristled as he listened. Lucy heard something too. The sound was raspy, yet steady, and it was getting louder by the moment—as if something that could not be seen was in the room with them, breathing heavily.

Lucy leapt to her feet, startling Mr. Mews, who ran back out of the room. She spun in a circle, searching the dark corners for shadowy figures. She saw nothing, but felt it all around her: a presence that was growing stronger and more intrusive with every breath. A sickly sweet smell, like strawberries and medicine, permeated the air. Lucy backed out of the room slowly, then turned on her heel and ran up the stairs, taking two at a time. She grabbed a small suitcase from the hall closet and filled it with random toiletries and clothing, and then quickly changed. Mismatched and untucked, Lucy hurried back downstairs to discover that the strange smell had grown even stronger; it nearly choked her as she ran to the kitchen and filled three bowls with cat food and a giant mixing bowl with water for Mr. Mews.

"It's teatime." A deep voice spoke from behind her.

Lucy turned around. The voice belonged to a man with heavy

eyebrows that nearly disguised his eyes, dressed in a butler's uniform and holding a tray with a silver tea set. She backed away from him and into the front hallway where she almost tripped over a woman wearing a maid's uniform mopping something red and syrupy off the floor. She was humming softly to herself as she worked. Without uttering a word, Lucy picked up her purse and keys and rushed out the door, locking it tightly behind her.

During the train ride back to New York City, Lucy considered the best way to break the news to her father. There was no way around it now; he had to know. She figured that his response would likely involve him moving in for a while to witness the disturbances for himself, or he would simply want to sell. There was a third option too, which involved her being committed to a psychiatric ward, but that thought was too upsetting to dwell on.

When Lucy arrived home, she was relieved to find that her father was out. She retreated to the safety of her old bedroom and, while she waited, immersed herself in daytime television and ate from a sleeve of saltines. She felt as if she had withdrawn inside herself, like a crustacean hiding in the safety of its own shell. Hours later, while lulled into a shallow soap opera–induced trance, Lucy heard her father's voice in the hallway.

"Lucy? Is that you?"

Lucy bolted up and wiped the cracker dust to the floor. She turned off the TV and tried to straighten out the bedsheets. The door swung open.

"What are you doing here?" Her father sounded more concerned than happy to see her.

"I thought I would come home for a visit," Lucy said, trying to act natural.

"Are you okay? You look exhausted." His six-foot frame filled the doorway.

"I'm fine."

"Really? You don't seem fine. What's going on?" he said, crossing his arms.

"Something is going on in the house," Lucy said meekly.

"Something is going on in the house?" Her father repeated her words, only louder and deeper. "What does that mean?"

"Strange things have been appearing: an ugly chair, weird food, then footsteps, and a man—"

"A man?" His face flashed with concern.

"Then a butler and a maid."

"What? What are you talking about?"

"I know it sounds crazy, but it's true."

"Have you taken something?" he said as he stepped inside her room and looked around. "Drugs? Mushrooms? Have you been binge-watching Downton Abbey again?"

"No." Lucy sank further into her bed, half hoping it would just swallow her up.

"This is a joke though, right?"

"No. Dad, it's not. I'm serious. I didn't want to tell you at first, but it began a few weeks after I moved in. It started with furniture magically appearing and disappearing, and then people started showing up."

"Showing up? What does that mean? Who are these people?"

"I don't know, but I don't think they're real. It's like they're ghosts or something."

His face contorted. "Ghosts?"

"I know, it sounds insane. But they may not be ghosts, and it might be just a witch thing."

"A witch thing? What are you talking about? Are you having a psychotic break?"

Lucy picked up a piece of cracker from her bed and crumbled it in her hand.

"Maybe." It was the first time she had considered it a distinct possibility.

He sat down on the edge of her bed and asked her to start at the beginning. She told him the entire story—from the bunny chair to the ugly cake that he himself had witnessed, to the French Braids and even the Room of Curiosities. By the time Lucy was finished she was exhausted, but also enormously relieved. Her eyelids felt heavy and she just wanted to sleep.

"Okay. Okay." Her father took in a deep breath as he collected his thoughts, and then exhaled loudly through his nose. "First off, stop this talk of witches and ghosts and nonsense. That's absurd. There is no such thing. And you carrying on like this is scaring the hell out of me. It's far more likely that someone is doing this deliberately. But the question is why. Who benefits from this? Tomorrow, first thing, I'm going to call that shrew of a realtor. If anyone has been trying to scare you, it's likely her. What did you say? She's sold that house over seventeen times? That's ridiculous. It's a scam, Lucy.

Some insane small-town scam. I'll call my lawyer in the morning too. You're exhausted. Try to get some sleep and I'm sure tomorrow you will see things more clearly." He patted her shoulder as he turned off the light and closed the door behind him.

In the darkness of her childhood bedroom, Lucy's thoughts drifted back to when she was a young girl. Her father had wanted her to be self-reliant, so on her eleventh birthday, they took the subway to an outer borough and he handed her a cellphone, map, bottle of water, and enough money for the return fare. Then he left, and she navigated herself home. They repeated this procedure for several weeks until Lucy was confident riding the subway by herself. She had never been frightened, but on occasion she'd felt resentful when watching other parents chaperoning their daughters on shopping trips or to the latest Broadway musical; these were families who clearly preferred to spend their weekends enjoying themselves rather than partaking in survivalist adventures. But upon Lucy's return, her efforts were always rewarded with lunch at a fancy restaurant where waiters wore ankle-length white aprons and refilled their water glasses every two minutes. The life lessons continued when she turned fourteen and her father enrolled her in a self-defense class that used hand-to-hand combat techniques. She still knew how to throw a decent throat punch. But what use was a throat punch in the face of magic? Or was it magic? Her father's voice of reason had started to sway her. Could it all have been a dreadful Scooby-Doo-style scam cooked up by the same person who tried to poison her? Anger began to percolate.

The next morning Lucy woke to the smell of freshly brewed coffee. She showered and changed and met her father in the kitchen.

"Lucy, I couldn't get a hold of that realtor, but I spoke to my lawyer. He's got a few tricks up his sleeve. I think he can get us out of the sale."

Lucy thought she would feel relieved, but instead she just felt defeated.

"But aren't we going to fight her? I love that house. I don't think we should just give in. I thought about it last night. Maybe if we bought some surveillance equipment, we could catch her in the act."

"No way. I'm not spending another dime on that place. I'm going to get all my money back, with interest," her father said sharply. "Don't worry, we'll find you a suitable studio apartment near the school."

Lucy knew that when her father made his mind up there was no point in arguing with him.

"Now, let's go find that elusive taco truck on the East Side that makes the best churros in the city. Let's make a day of it. What do you say?" He rubbed his hands together enthusiastically.

"Sure," Lucy replied, unenthusiastically.

"Great. But first I'm going to run to the store and pick up a few things. We're out of truffle oil, if you can believe it. I can also swing by Smithfields to pick up those iced breakfast buns that you like. Need anything else?" he said as he grabbed his keys and sunglasses.

Lucy shook her head, and her father left to run his errands. His solution to trauma often involved butter, sugar, and salt, but the last thing Lucy felt like doing was eating a breakfast bun.

Breakfast buns. Lucy repeated the words in her head. *Buns . . . Bun-Bun . . . Clover Rose.*

"The rabbits!" Lucy shouted into the empty room.

It was the day that Brenda and Marigold were leaving for the cottage, and Lucy realized that they'd neglected to exchange phone numbers. With no reasonable way to get in touch with them, Lucy eagerly decided to take it as a sign: she had to go back to Esther Wren.

CHAPTER NINE

Shenanigans

The clarity that Lucy had experienced in New York had begun to cloud by the time the scenery from the train window changed from construction sites to cornfields. It had all seemed so simple earlier: Millicent was scaring them out of the house for the sake of a commission. But there were still so many things that didn't add up. Even if Millicent had hired a cast of actors to run around her house, it couldn't explain the footsteps that walked right past her in the living room, not to mention the entire contents of the Room of Curiosities. She knew her father would just describe them as parlor tricks—smoke and mirrors—nothing that a birthday-party magician couldn't easily conjure up. But Lucy's intuition told her otherwise. Lucy allowed her growing belief to take shape in her mind: Magic was real. And there were witches living in her town— maybe even next door!

By the time the train pulled into Esther Wren, Lucy was ready for anything Millicent chose to throw at her. She took note of the weather: sunny and warm with a slight breeze. The heat wave had passed, likely driven out by the windstorm. It was a perfect day for a walk. Lucy took the long route home, passing by the lake and stopping at the Turner Inn for lunch. It was there, while she sat under a canary-yellow umbrella, that she sensed something unusual about the day. Although there appeared to be the normal volume of tourists milling about, drifting in and out of shops, enjoying ice cream cones, there seemed to be fewer locals. The hot dog stand was closed, the town troubadour was absent from his usual spot by the fountain, and there was plenty of parking in front of the bank. When the waiter returned with her bill, Lucy asked if there was something special going on—like a fair, or a town hall meeting—but he just shrugged his shoulders, as if he hadn't noticed anything out of the ordinary.

Lucy headed home, taking Charles Avenue over to Oak Grove, where some of the loveliest gardens in town resided. She walked along the sidewalk, lingering longer in the shady patches, admiring the rosebushes in riotous palettes of red, pink, yellow, and mauve. They spilled out over fences, showy and untamed, perfuming the air with their spicy-sweet scent. She understood that such inflated beauty was likely the result of witchcraft, but that didn't lessen its allure.

The shade gave way as Lucy turned onto her street and was forced into the blazing light of the early afternoon. She squinted and saw a mass of people, at least a hundred, standing on the sidewalk and street, just about where her house was located. There was also an out-of-town news van and a police car parked at the side of the road. A surge of adrenaline immediately shot through her. As she approached the crowd of spectators, they turned and cast their eyes downward and politely moved out of her way, allowing her passage to her property. She prepared herself for the worst—a fire or a flood—but she was rendered speechless at the sight of a vacant lot.

Lucy stared at the empty expanse of grass where her house had once stood. Her hands trembled and her mouth went dry. When she was finally able to speak again, her words scraped against her throat.

"Where is it?" she asked softly.

No one answered.

She took a few steps toward her property.

"Where is it?" she asked again, her voice louder and more panicked.

Lucy walked down the cement pathway that normally led to her front steps. To the left was the lilac tree and to the right were the evergreens, but in front of her, in the spot where her house had once stood, there was only a blanket of scrubby yellow grass dotted with leaves and broken tree branches. The only structure that remained was the crumbling greenhouse at the far corner of her property. Lucy bent down and ran her fingers over the lawn. Every blade of grass stood straight on end, as if it had always been that way, as if her house had never existed. Cautiously, Lucy took a step onto the grass, and then another and another until she was standing in the place that was once her living room. Lucy brought her hands up to her mouth and tried to suppress a cry of disbelief. Her mind raced. *Where did it go? How did this happen? What—or who—did this? Mr. Mews! Where are you?*

Lucy's mind searched for a reasonable explanation: a tornado? But where was all the debris? Lucy looked toward her neighbors' houses. They stood intact—not even a stray shingle. It was no tornado. Suddenly, a reporter with bright pink lipstick and an artificial smile stepped in front of her.

"Julie Blue of Syracuse Channel 8 news here. Do you mind if I ask you a few questions?"

Lucy pushed past her and began walking back toward the sidewalk. She walked to the end of her property and sat down on the edge of her suitcase and stared over to Mr. Holland's perfectly symmetrical boxwood hedges. She saw his living room curtains close. She sat still for several minutes, trying to comprehend this most recent twist of events. What would have happened to her if she had been inside her house when it vanished? Where would she be? Would she exist in another dimension? Would she exist at all? A man behind her cleared his throat loudly. It was Brian Norton—the police officer from the other day—still sweaty and doughy in his tight blue uniform.

"Miss, are you the owner of the house?"

"Yes. Well, technically my dad is, but he's in New York. I live here. We met the other day when I tried to file a report about an intruder in my kitchen. My name is Lucy Crisp—remember?"

The officer stared at her with a furrowed brow until a look of recognition fell across his face.

"Oh yes! You're the girl who was upset about the picnic in her dining room."

"No, it wasn't a picnic. That was a stranger—"

"Miss Crisp, can you tell me when your house disappeared?" Officer Brian interrupted.

"Well, it must have been within the past twenty-four hours. When I left yesterday morning, it was fine, but now it's gone—obviously."

"Would you be able to identify it in a lineup?"

"What?"

Officer Brian Norton chuckled. "Oh, that's just a little cop humor."

Lucy's lack of enthusiasm for jokes about her missing home prompted Officer Norton to sullenly jot down a detailed description of the house on a notepad, as if he were filling out a missing person's report. He left her with a very limp reassurance that they would get to the bottom of its disappearance.

Lucy took a deep breath and tried to ignore the whispers and shuffles from the gawkers.

"Wasn't sure if you might be needing these." Lucy looked up and saw Mr. Holland standing next to her, with a sleeping bag, folding lawn chair, and a flashlight.

"Oh, thanks," Lucy said, realizing that she might very well be spending the night camped out in her greenhouse.

"You didn't happen to see my cat, did you?" Lucy asked.

"No, sorry," Mr. Holland replied. "But if it's any consolation, there was another house in town that used to disappear also."

"Used to?" Lucy asked, hopeful that maybe there was a cure.

"About thirty years ago or so. I had just moved here with my wife and kids, so I wasn't paying too much attention to the shenanigans in this town." He paused. "You do know about the shenanigans?"

Lucy nodded. She was all too familiar with the town's shenanigans.

"Anyway, rumor had it that there was this house over on Oak Grove that was prone to disappearing. At first it was just for a few days, you know, but then it up and disappeared for nearly a month. Then, the day after it reappeared, it blew up."

"Blew up?"

"That's right. Pow!" He smacked his hands together dramatically. "We had just sat down for dinner when we felt the explosion. The impact caused one of my wife's cuckoo clocks to fall off the wall. The fire department said it was a gas leak. I guess with all that disappearing and reappearing, something didn't get connected properly. Such a shame too. It was a big old white house with four columns at the front. A real beauty— just like yours." He shook his head and sighed. "Well, I best be on my way. If you need to use the bathroom, just knock." He handed her the sleeping bag, set up the lawn chair, and gave her a light pat on the shoulder before he left.

Just like yours.

Lucy remembered Eugenia's statement, about another house with a lovely porch. Could that have been the house Eugenia was referring to? Another disappearing house? Lucy moved over to the lawn chair. She pulled a package of trail mix from her purse and contemplated her latest predicament. One thing was for certain: she was going to contact the gas company as soon as her house returned.

It wasn't until late afternoon that the reality of being homeless began to sink in. The initial shock had worn off and practical thoughts were beginning to weigh on her: Should she call her father? Was the greenhouse really suitable for habitation? She thought about her typewriter and her silly half-written stories and wondered if they were lost forever. Lucy checked her watch. It was getting close to five o'clock—time to feed Marigold's rabbits.

When she returned to her property, she discovered that a second wave of gawkers had arrived on the street. Many came in the guise of dog walkers, but Lucy recognized only a handful of dogs from the neighborhood. One particularly docile cocker spaniel suddenly snapped as it passed Lucy's property—lunging toward it, choking at the end of its leash—snarling and barking until its flustered owner had to pick it up and carry it away.

Then the children came. They gathered in packs, some on bikes, others on foot, daring each other to step on the lawn. One boy, accepting a dare, ran out onto the grass as fast as he could, circling the spot where her house had once stood, and returned boasting to the others of his bravery. At dusk, Lucy experienced the teenagers. They idled in cars with windows open and stereos blasting—some snickering, some just glassy-eyed and speechless. One guy in a black Honda stopped in front of where Lucy was sitting and yelled out, "Dude, where's your house?"

"It's missing," Lucy replied, not really wanting to engage in a conversation.

"That sucks. What did it look like?" he yelled back, sounding genuinely interested.

"It's white, and the architectural style is Second Empire. It has a tower at the front."

"A tower? Cool! Like in *Lord of the Rings*?"

"Not really."

"Okay, I'll keep an eye out for a Second Umpire with a tower. I don't think it could have gone very far."

He had a point. Logically, how could it have gone very far? How could something so big just disappear without a trace? Lucy pondered that thought until the streetlights came on and parents called out for their children to come inside. Within minutes, the lively neighborhood noises evaporated into a dull murmur of crickets. Lucy checked her phone to find a string of concerned texts and emails from her father asking her why she'd left. She texted back and told him she was fine and that they would talk tomorrow. Lucy turned off her phone for the evening and decided to take Mr. Holland up on his offer to use his bathroom. After being in his house for only a few minutes, she realized that her suspicions about him were unwarranted. There were no signs of domestic devilry—or any sort of devilry, for that matter. He was a kind man, still heartbroken over the death of his wife, but very talkative about his love of books and his grandchildren. Lucy asked him about his unusual grass-cutting attire. He laughed, agreeing that it was an odd habit, and then explained that his wife had suffered from terrible grass allergies; he wore his bathing suit when he cut the grass and hosed himself off before he entered the house. It was a ritual that, in spite of his wife's passing, he just couldn't abandon. He offered her a plate of cold pork chops and his daughter's old bedroom until her house returned. Lucy happily accepted the pork chops but politely declined the room. She had a natural independence, and she wanted to impose as little as possible. He gave her a set of fresh towels, a bar of soap, and a key to the house so she could use the bathroom whenever she needed.

That night Lucy slept on the floor of her greenhouse wrapped in Mr. Holland's sleeping bag that smelled like a hundred wet camping trips. She had a dream that her house was floating above her like a hot air balloon. A string of pots and pans dangled from it, and just as Lucy took hold of the string, the wind blew, and she was lifted up into the sky. Tethered to her house, Lucy glided past rooftops and chimneys while watching the townspeople below as they busied themselves with the routine events of their daily lives—taking no notice of the girl in the sky. She sailed above the park, and then over the lake, where her house descended just enough so she could skim the tips of her toes along the water. As she approached Ladywyck Lodge, the sky dimmed to night and her house soared up into the flickering stars. Lucy reached out to touch one; it felt thin and silvery, like tinfoil, and then it broke apart in her hand, covering her arm in a thin layer of glitter.

Down below, the witches of Ladywyck had begun to gather on the lawn. They lit a great bonfire that hissed and spat sparks into the sky. The sparks tickled Lucy's feet, making her laugh, and she heard someone else's laughter mimicking her own. That was when Lucy realized she wasn't alone in the sky. A short distance away, a woman hovered in the air—free and wild-looking with flowing white hair and a beautiful face. The woman spoke to her without opening her mouth. She asked Lucy what she was doing in the sky, to which Lucy replied that she was trying to pull her house back down to the ground. The woman told her that she didn't belong and that she should go. Lucy asked her how she was able to fly, and the woman explained that she was meant for the sky: it was her birthright. She was a banshee, a foreseer of death, and she had a message to deliver to the dying, but she didn't want to. It was such a burden giving bad news. She let out a sorrowful moan, and then another, working

herself up until she let loose a wail so powerful that it cracked all the windows in Lucy's house. Shards of glass rained down upon them, causing Lucy to lose her grip on the string, and as she fell to ground, she could hear the banshee apologizing for her outburst. She couldn't help it, she said. It was just her nature.

———

Lucy jolted awake with the banshee wail, shrill and haunting, still ringing in her ears. The sun was just beginning to rise, casting the morning in a moody violet glow. Lucy looked up through the dusty glass ceiling and searched the sky for remnants of her dream, but it was already fading away. By the time she climbed to her feet and dusted herself off, the dream had disappeared almost entirely from memory. She headed over to Brenda's house to check on the rabbits, and then over to Mr. Holland's to shower and change and hopefully get a strong cup of coffee. When she returned to her property, she discovered that her mail had arrived in exactly the same spot where her mailbox used to be. A canvas hamper had also appeared near the edge of the sidewalk with a sign attached that read *Quill House Donations*. It was a quarter full with various canned goods, a box of soda crackers, two Granny Smith apples, one can of ginger ale, a bottle of sunscreen, an old board game, and two dog chew toys.

Lucy settled into the lawn chair with one of the apples from the homeless hamper and watched as a black truck pulled up in front of Mr. Holland's house. It was an unusual-looking vehicle, possibly a catering truck in a previous life, before it had been refurbished with glossy black paint and the name Ghost Charmers painted along the

158

side. A redhead in skinny jeans and a straw fedora jumped out of the driver's side holding a wand-like gadget, earphones, and a laptop. He smiled at Lucy as he trespassed onto her property and began pointing the wand at the ground. He moved quickly around her lawn, back and forth, almost as if he were performing a dance, pausing every so often to type on his laptop and text on his phone. Lucy wondered if she should introduce herself but was overwhelmed with indifference. She had much bigger things to be concerned about than the shenanigans of a hipster ghost charmer.

She took a bite of her apple and watched as her street began to wake up. One by one, people appeared in their doorways and driveways, collecting mail, turning on sprinklers, and heading off to work. It appeared that everyone was attempting to get on with their lives and pretend that they couldn't see the homeless girl eating an apple on a borrowed lawn chair. She'd figured this would happen eventually, but was surprised it had happened so quickly. Then, Lucy saw a white Cadillac with tinted windows inching its way down her street. It crawled to a stop right in front of where she was sitting and idled menacingly. Lucy stood up and walked over to the car, stopping just short of the curb. The driver's-side window rolled down and a waft of cigarette smoke violated the fresh morning air.

"Looks like you need a new house," Millicent said as she waved her business card out the window. "I can schedule you in at 4 p.m. tomorrow. There's a lovely Craftsman-style bungalow available, a rare find in these parts. Might be a little more manageable for you."

Lucy felt her face grow hot with anger.

"Are you joking?"

"Joking? Why would I want to do that?" Millicent asked, appearing insulted at the suggestion that she had a sense of humor.

"Millicent, you sold us a house that disappeared! And not only that, when it was here, it was haunted. You're the last person I would ever hire to be my realtor."

Lucy watched as Millicent's thin red lips pursed and her eyes narrowed into small black marbles. Her instinct was to get out of the way before Millicent could work her magic on her again, but she was distracted by the sight of Midgely dressed in a long white nightgown walking along the sidewalk in her bare feet. She moved calmly but with purpose. She passed Lucy without uttering a word and went out onto the road, stopping just short of the hood of Millicent's Cadillac. Sensing something was about to happen, Lucy backed away nervously.

At first Millicent seemed more curious than bothered with the young, tawny-haired roadblock. She even lit a cigarette and eased back into her seat while she studied Midgely. But her impatience soon got the better of her and she leaned on the car horn—long and loud, like a battle cry.

Midgely didn't flinch.

"Get out of my way!" Millicent shouted out the window, revving her engine.

Midgely responded by placing her hands on her hips and cocking her head forward in a gesture that could only be interpreted as "make me."

"Get out of my way, you stupid twit, or I'll use you like a speed bump!"

Midgely continued to stand her ground. Somewhere off in the distance, Lucy heard the tinkling of wind chimes.

Millicent climbed out of the car, leaving the door open, and walked over to Midgely, stopping only a foot away from her. She whispered something to Midgely that made the girl's body stiffen. Lucy felt the temperature drop, and her arms tingled with goose bumps. Then a sudden gust of wind blew so hard that it caused Millicent to stagger backward and the car door to slam shut. Lucy looked around to see if anyone else was watching and realized that all of her neighbors had disappeared from their front lawns and driveways. The only witness to the exchange was the hipster ghost charmer, who was recording it on his phone.

It took Millicent a few seconds to regain her composure. She adjusted her almond-colored blazer and patted her hair smooth. Then she smiled a hating smile at Midgely and sputtered out a few more coughs.

"Is that the best you can do, weather girl? I've got more wind than you after you eat your grandmother's pot roast."

"Leave her out of this," Midgely snapped back.

The wind suddenly became more volatile—shifting directions, tearing leaves and small branches off trees, and whipping up grit from the road.

"Why? Isn't that what this is all about? The fact that your grandmother is my maid? But don't worry; you'll get your chance too. I'm actually in need of someone who can scrub a toilet better than she can. Those arthritic hands of hers are becoming a problem," Millicent taunted.

"Why don't you go back to Ladywyck and bake a few pies. I hear you're missed there," Midgely spat back.

Lucy looked down at her half-eaten apple, its edges beginning to brown, and thought about Millicent's award-wining apple-head doll.

Millicent squinted at Midgely and the wind instantly dropped. An eerie stillness settled in. Millicent took a long drag of her cigarette and exhaled a thin ribbon of smoke.

Suddenly, Midgely began to retch. She grasped her jaw and doubled over. Millicent, a sly smile appearing in the corner of her mouth, continued to smoke as she observed Midgely. Lucy's instinct was to help Midgely, but she thought better of it when she noticed that the girl's sisters were watching from their front porch. The fact that they seemed unconcerned for their sister's safety was a slight reassurance to Lucy.

Midgely recovered quickly. She straightened herself up, took a few deep breaths, and spat out what appeared to be a tooth.

"Oh dear. It looks as if someone isn't practicing proper oral hygiene. I guess there's no one to teach you such things, with your parents absent most of the time, struggling to make ends meet, and your poor grandmother working night and day for me." Millicent started to laugh, which threw her into a coughing fit. "And yes, your grandmother won a few battles in her day, but her spells were always weak as tea. I look back at my stint at Ladywyck as a pleasant vacation."

"It was a long vacation. I heard she turned you into a Goodie for four years." Midgely smirked as a thin trickle of blood slid down her chin, staining the collar of her nightgown.

Millicent took a few steps toward Midgely and narrowed her eyes. On cue, Midgely doubled over again and spat out another tooth.

"I could go on like this all day. How many teeth does the average idiot girl have in her head?"

Midgely sank to her knees and clutched her mouth.

"Like I said, your grandmother won a few fights, but guess what, Missy?" Millicent dropped her cigarette and ground it into the pavement with the tip of her shoe until it was nothing more than a black smudge. "I won the war. Now go clean yourself up. You look a fright."

Millicent walked back to her car triumphantly. But just as she reached for the door handle, a gust of wind came at her, tearing the wig from her head and sending it high into the trees. Bald Millicent stood stunned, her mouth agape, and before she had a chance to locate her wig, she was hit hard by another gust of wind. It was violent and whip-fast; the force of it knocked her off her feet and sent her rolling like tumbleweed until she hit the far curb. A cry of alarm came from one of the neighboring houses, followed by the distant wail of a police siren. Time seemed to stand still as Millicent lay motionless in the street—like expensively dressed roadkill. Midgely made her way to Millicent and stood over her for several seconds, observing the realtor's prone form carefully as she wiped her bloody mouth on the back of her hand and sighed. It was long and drawn out—satisfied sounding. Then she turned around and headed back toward her house. As she passed, drenched in sweat and clearly exhausted, she shot Lucy a triumphant look.

The ambulance was the first to arrive on the scene, followed by a police car. The paramedics rushed over to Millicent, but as soon as they

began to examine her, she jerked awake and swatted them away like flies. They took several steps back and monitored her from a distance, uncertain of what to do. The police officer sat in his car, watching Millicent as she climbed to her feet and stumbled around on one shoe. Her nylons were shredded and her wool suit covered in scuff marks. Eventually, he got out of his car and cautiously walked a few steps toward Millicent. Lucy noticed that it was the same officer who had filed the report on her missing house.

"Go away, Brian," Millicent barked.

"Listen, Millicent, I have to file a report on this."

"Oh, go stuff your report. The only thing you need to report is that the oldest Drummond girl is nuts. She should be put in a cage, along with the rest of her feral sisters."

"Did she start this?" Officer Brian asked.

"You know better than to get involved," Millicent growled. "Shouldn't you be doing something better with your time—like dealing with that silly girl?" Millicent turned and pointed a long tobacco-stained finger at Lucy. "Go find her missing house, why don't you? Or, better yet, stop that rabbity-looking creature from filming this. It's an invasion of my privacy. If this ends up on the internet, there will be hell to pay!" Millicent said, shouting out the last few words as a threat.

The officer looked over at the ghost charmer, who instantly pulled his phone protectively to his chest. Lucy could see that his hand was shaking badly.

"Actually, on second thought, you could put your detective skills to work and find my other shoe," Millicent instructed. "It's around here somewhere."

Officer Brian nodded obediently. He found the shoe lodged deeply in Mr. Holland's boxwood hedges. Millicent tore it from his hand.

Then, Officer Brian motioned upward. Millicent's wig was dangling from a branch.

"I assume you're not going to crawl up that tree to get it, so call the damn fire department. And have it sent to my office."

Millicent hobbled back to her car, eased herself gingerly into the driver's seat, and slammed the door. She proceeded to make an awkward three-point turn and then slowly left, heading back in the same direction from which she'd come.

CHAPTER TEN

Cats

Lucy had witnessed a witch fight, and she wasn't entirely sure what to make of it. Everything had happened so quickly that she could almost convince herself she'd imagined it all. But then she spied Midgely's teeth lying in the middle of the road. They were bright white and healthy-looking—glistening in a small puddle of blood. There was also a strange smell that lingered in the air, like rotting vegetables and burnt metal. Lucy looked over at the ghost charmer. He was leaning up against a tree, his skin ashen, taking deep puffs from his asthma inhaler.

Officer Brian approached her. "Miss Crisp, I understand that you witnessed what happened." His voice was deep and serious.

Lucy nodded apprehensively.

"Well, I would appreciate it if you would keep quiet about what you saw. I'm sure you can imagine how easily things can get blown out of proportion. Idle chatter leads to rumors, and rumors lead to mass hysteria. Before you know it, house prices plummet, the FBI gets called in, and religious fanatics appear on every corner. Nothing good will come of it, I can assure you."

Startled by the rather dramatic series of events Officer Brian had prophesied, Lucy decided it would be easiest if she just agreed to keep it to herself.

"I also wanted to let you know that we are working very hard on finding out what happened to your house. We're bringing the Trumbo triplets in for questioning this morning."

"The Trumbo triplets?"

"Brothers. All seventeen years old. It's been a long, hot summer, and this time of year we usually have dealings with them. If you end up with a pizza guy at your door with twenty anchovy pizzas, then you know you've been Trumboed." Officer Brian chuckled to himself.

"You think some teenage pranksters are behind this—really? There's a big difference between twenty pizzas and making a house vanish into thin air."

"Well, right now, it's our best lead," he said defensively.

"Considering what just happened here, I can't help but think there's a little more to it," Lucy said, gesturing at the broken tree branches scattered across the road.

"Can't say I know what you're getting at."

"You know—magic."

"Magic? Well, that sounds like crazy talk," he said as he looked over Lucy's shoulder.

"Good morning, Mrs. Morrison!" Officer Brian shouted.

Lucy turned to see the birdhouse lady coming toward them. She was wearing slippers, and her hair was set in plastic pink rollers.

"Hello, Officer!" Mrs. Morrison responded in a thick New Jersey accent as she went onto the road and scoured the pavement carefully. She suddenly crouched down and removed a tissue from her pocket. Very gently, she placed the teeth into the tissue and slid it back into her pocket.

"Mrs. Morrison, what are you doing?" Officer Brian shouted.

"Nothing to worry about, Officer," Mrs. Morrison said dismissively as she hurried back to the sidewalk.

"That's evidence! Put them back!"

The birdhouse lady quickened her pace. Officer Brian excused himself from Lucy and hurried after her.

He lowered his voice. "Don't you be selling those on the black market. I know you're auctioning a lot more than just birdhouses on the internet."

Officer Brian lumbered along, breathless, pleading for Mrs. Morrison to hand over the teeth, but his entreaties were met with a door slammed in his face. He paced back and forth on her front stoop before eventually giving up and returning to the scene of the incident. Lucy watched as he scoured the pavement, possibly searching for more teeth. Suddenly, a squirrel darted past him and then up the tree that Millicent's wig dangled from. The squirrel began to pick at the wig as Officer Brian did his best to shoo it away with sticks and pebbles.

Lucy returned to her lawn chair. Just as she began to wonder what she was going to do with the rest of her day, aside from being a spectator to Officer Brian's pebble tossing and the ghost charmer's wand dance, she spotted Scarlett coming toward her carrying an oversized basket of produce.

"Lucy! I just heard about your house. I'm so sorry! I brought you a few things from my garden," Scarlett said as she presented the basket. Lucy peered in to discover an assortment of deformed-looking vegetables.

"They're mostly experiments, but all perfectly edible. My favorite is the spicy cucumber." Scarlett pointed toward a pale and somewhat deflated cucumber. "It starts out tasting a lot like a cucumber, but then the flavor shifts into something more peppery. And then it starts to get hot . . . and hotter . . . until it feels like your tongue is about to burn off! I've also included my milk radishes; they taste a lot like blue cheese. Those aren't for everybody, though. People either love them or hate them."

"Thanks, Scarlett. That's very thoughtful," Lucy said as she placed the basket by the homeless hamper, trying her best not to stare too long at its strange contents.

"So, what are you going to do?" Scarlett asked.

"I thought I would go to the library to do some research on my house. I also thought I would stop by Eugenia Forrester's place. At the Potluck Pottery Social, I got the feeling she knows something about my house."

"Listen, I have a better idea," Scarlett said. "Come with me."

"Where to?" Lucy asked as she grabbed her purse.

"It's time to get you some real answers."

They headed east, and it wasn't long before Lucy recognized the neighborhood that she'd discovered when she followed the French Braids after leaving the supermarket.

"What is this place?" Lucy asked Scarlett.

"We call it Old Town. But when I think about it, I don't think it's really any older than the rest of the town. A lot of Goodies live in this area. I think it has something to do with the energy," she said as she drew in a deep breath. "At night, they have these big parties with live music, and they light bonfires. It's awesome."

"There is something special about this place."

"You can feel it too, huh?" Scarlett asked.

"Yes, I think I can."

They continued on for several blocks until they reached a vintage clothing shop just off Main Street, located in a yellow Georgian-style house with a circular pea-gravel driveway. In the middle of the driveway stood a gnarled oak tree with vintage clothing and purses in sherbet colors dangling like fruit from every branch.

"Welcome to Emerald's Closet!" Scarlett announced with pride. "Emerald is my aunt. Her shop is on the first floor. She has the best vintage clothing in the state. She's also the best Clair in the state, which is why I brought you here."

"Clair?" Lucy asked.

"Clairvoyant. Did you not see her card in the welcome basket? It's green and pink."

Lucy's mind quickly went over the contents of the basket.

"Good Witch Services?" she asked.

Scarlett nodded. "It's one of her side businesses."

"I thought it was a cleaning service," Lucy explained, feeling quite silly. "I didn't know then that witches actually existed."

"It does take some getting used to," Scarlett said as she patted Lucy's arm reassuringly.

Suddenly, a woman emerged from the doorway dressed in a lavender shift dress and a matching silk scarf reminiscent of a 1960s flight attendant uniform.

"Aunt Em, you have to change your business card. People around here think you run a maid service," Scarlett told the woman as she gave her a hug.

"Is that so?" the woman responded as her eyes diverted to Lucy. "You must be Lucy."

"I am." Lucy smiled and extended her hand.

Emerald squeezed Lucy's hand warmly with both of her own.

"I'm surprised that it's taken us this long to meet—although you did bike past me the day of that terrible storm. Your lovely indigo-blue dress caught my attention. I was going to introduce myself, but you seemed to be on a mission."

"I was on my way to see my realtor, Millicent Brown," Lucy responded, offering up Millicent's name just to see what Emerald's reaction would be.

"And how did that go?" Emerald asked.

"Not very well."

"Well, you seem to have all your limbs intact."

"Yes, but I think she tried to poison me with a cookie."

"That sounds more like her," Emerald said as she led Lucy inside. "Although usually there is a motive to her madness. Did you do anything to rile her up?" Emerald asked.

"I tried to get out of the house sale."

"So, you threatened her money," Emerald said, making a *tsk–tsk* sound with her teeth. "Millicent's spell of choice is a Louisiana Vile. Did the room get really humid?"

"Yes, it did, come to think of it."

"Did you feel nauseous? Head spins? Hallucinations?"

"Yes—very nauseous." Just the thought of it was making Lucy feel queasy again.

"Sounds like a Louisiana Vile—also what some refer to as 'fascination' or the evil eye. It's fast-acting and requires little effort for an accomplished witch—just brief eye contact. Millicent tends to use it as a distraction spell, although the humidity factor can be a tip-off. But at least there's hardly any smell."

"Smell?"

"Oh, Lucy, you have a lot to learn." She led Lucy inside and over to the sales counter, which was covered in a heap of clothing and jewelry and topped with two sleeping velvety-gray cats.

"Lipswitch and Beauty! Get off!" Emerald hollered at them. "I turn my back for just a second and they appear, and always on the merchandise." The two cats lazily looked up at Emerald and then, in unison, vaulted off the counter and disappeared.

"Care for some tea? I have a lovely Lapsang souchong. It's smoky and slightly bitter, but I sweeten it with lavender honey."

"No, thank you. I'm fine," Lucy replied, feeling too hot to drink tea and a little wary of the beverage since her experience at Millicent's.

Scarlett appeared with a pile of dresses and gave a sheepish smile to her aunt as she closed the green velvet curtain to the change room.

"I've had some experience with your house over the years,"

Emerald said. "It has a history. I have to give you credit, though—you have outstayed everyone else. Most people leave in a matter of weeks. But I can tell you are a determined young woman." Emerald smiled.

"A police officer told me that it was likely some pranksters. Possibly the Trumbo triplets."

Emerald rolled her eyes. "It's not the Trumbo triplets, I can assure you. Mind you, they can make a decent stink bomb, but making a house disappear is a little out of their league. Although there are three of them, they share only one brain," Emerald said as she carefully arranged some pearls in a glass display case. "No, the cause of the disappearance is supernatural."

"Supernatural—as in haunted?"

"Not quite. Your house is enchanted."

Lucy thought about the Room of Curiosities. "Is there a difference?"

"There certainly is. Enchantments are quite different from hauntings. Very rarely is a house haunted. Most household disturbances are usually rotting floorboards, old plumbing, and mice. Although there can be other legitimate reasons. In fact, I just had Ellis Tott in here about an hour ago. For years, he's been complaining about his haunted shed. I kept telling him that he didn't have ghosts, he has fairies."

"Fairies?" Lucy repeated.

"Uh-huh. No wonder, as his property backs on to Eugenia Forrester's estate. Do you know her?"

"Yes—she's the lady who makes that delicious fairy water."

"That's right. But don't drink that stuff. It will attract fairies to you, and you don't want that. The last thing you need is to be kidnapped by a fairy."

"But aren't fairies really tiny?"

"Exactly," Emerald said. "And that was what was throwing Ellis Tott off. He couldn't see them with that bad eyesight of his, so I kept telling him to get better glasses, which he just did, and now he has finally seen them. You see, in spite of all her complaints about fairies, Eugenia has created a very favorable environment for them. She has a large estate, with plenty of wooded areas. And then there's that darn maze. Fairies love a good maze. Anyway, at some point, they decided that they liked Ellis Tott's shed, and they use it for reproductive purposes."

"You mean they're mating?"

"They certainly are. Three days out of every month his shed shakes like no one's business. Of course, he thought the place was haunted." Emerald laughed. "He's broken more than a few brooms beating the evil out of that poor shed."

Lucy realized that Ellis Tott must have been the man in the straw hat, the one she saw hitting his garden shed that afternoon when she followed the French Braids.

"But back to your situation," Emerald said as she plugged in an electric kettle. "An enchantment is when an inanimate object—in your case, your house—has been given unnatural life. To be honest, a haunting is in some ways preferable to an enchantment because it's often more straightforward: a spirit usually has a motive behind its behavior. But an enchantment can be more puzzling as the explanation is usually less obvious." Emerald paused to examine the clasp on the back of a brooch. "I've been in your house several times and have never been able to figure out the source of the enchantment. But I will say this, an enchantment requires three things: a spell, an energy source, and a conduit."

A look of confusion washed over Lucy's face.

"I know. It's a lot to absorb. You see, a spell is essentially like a recipe. It needs ingredients—just as a loaf of bread will require flour, yeast, water, and sugar. But that bread isn't going to bake on its own unless you add the energy—or heat, so to speak. And in order to access that heat, you will need a conduit, like an oven. Of course, in magical terms, a conduit is often a talisman. And a talisman can be anything—well, likely not something as mundane as a coffee cup, but mirrors, paintings, decorative items, dolls, handmade things and the like. Jewelry, of course, is a common conduit," Emerald said as she held up a 1970s-style orange beaded necklace. "By the way, avoid all garage sales, yard sales, even church rummage sales in Esther Wren, if you know what's good for you. They are hotbeds for enchanted objects. The last thing you need is to buy a pretty oil painting of a sweet little Persian kitten only to discover the next day that you have a wildcat scratching all your good furniture to shreds."

At that moment, Lucy spotted the small sign by the cash register that read *100% Enchantment-Free Merchandise Guarantee.*

"But how do I figure out what the conduit is? Everything in my house is gone."

"It doesn't necessarily have to be *in* your house. It could technically be anywhere."

"But if you're clairvoyant, can't you just see what it is?"

"It doesn't work like that, unfortunately. I can't see everything. With most spells there are veils that hide their energy sources and conduits. And this veil is so thick that I'd almost consider it a wimple."

"Ta-da!" Scarlett whipped the dressing room curtain back and presented herself in an ivory 1960s-style minidress with a gold beaded neckline.

"Wow! You look amazing!" Lucy exclaimed.

"I don't look like a 1960s nightclub act?" Scarlett asked as she spun around. "I don't want Daniel to think it's too much."

"The dress isn't too much, but *he* is," Emerald said. "How many times do I have to tell you that he's not for you?" Scarlett's face instantly dropped, and she pulled the curtain closed.

"And for you, Lucy, I think this is your dress." Emerald held up a sleeveless summer dress with a full skirt and a scoop neckline patterned with sparrows. Lucy instantly adored it.

"I'll try it on."

"No need. I already know it will fit you perfectly and that you will love it for a long time." She winked as she pulled out some tissue paper to wrap it in.

"That will be sixty dollars, even."

"And for the information?"

Emerald appeared confused.

"Your business card said that this is a service, right? Good Witch Services? Isn't there a fee?"

"It's on the house." Emerald winked as she passed her the bag.

———

Famished from their visit with Emerald, Lucy and Scarlett stopped by Betty's Cupcake and Tea Palace, where they shared a "cupcake goodie plate"—a round-up of fifteen miniature cupcakes presented on a vintage cake stand. Lucy was desperate for a coffee, but the closest thing on the menu was a "coffee tea," which the waitress described as a strong black tea with a distinct coffee-like flavor. It was clear that Esther Wren was a tea drinkers' town. Scarlett explained that most Goodies disliked coffee, but the Baddies appreciated it—so much so that some believed it actually enhanced their abilities. There were a few diners and restaurants in town that served watered-down versions of coffee, but the real coffee houses were places that regular people generally avoided. The words "regular people" hung awkwardly in the air as the waitress presented them with their cupcake goodie plate.

"So, you just live out in the open?" Lucy asked.

"How else are we supposed to live?" Scarlett replied, sinking her teeth into a salted-caramel cupcake.

"I thought you would want to keep your identities secret."

Scarlett wiped her hands on her napkin, appearing to contemplate the idea of secret identities.

"Well, we don't go around broadcasting it, for obvious reasons. But this lifestyle is all I know. And most of my friends and family are like me—it's normal to us. It really isn't so different from someone who is really talented at, say, singing or dancing. I mean, where does an ability come from? Who's to say that isn't magic, right?"

"But Clementine Howard says that you're a different species."

"Is that the woman who wrote the Elle Mort series? I wanted to be just like Elle when I was thirteen. Then I realized that she was actually a Baddie. But she was so cool," Scarlett said wistfully. "But I haven't read Clementine Howard's nonfiction."

"Do you mind being called a witch?" Lucy asked. "I mean, I wouldn't want to use the wrong term and offend anyone."

Scarlett laughed. "It's fine. We're used to that word, but in our community we're defined more by our specific abilities. Like my aunt is seen as a Clair, and I see myself as a Grower."

"Have you had your magical powers all your life?"

"Well, I only really have the one ability, which, by the way, we prefer to call talents or abilities. But lately, it's not so much a talent as it is an embarrassment. The energy has been really off all summer, and I can't seem to harness it properly. But I would say I've had my talent all my life. If you can believe it, one of my first memories is of my parents weeding my nursery. My talent actually comes from my great-grandfather, who was a florist in New York City. But of course, back then, you really had to be very careful about using a talent. So he opened a little flower shop, and within a short time, he attracted a cult following of society ladies who couldn't get enough of his immortal orchids. After a while, they were on to him, but they kept his secret. Having the best flowers in the city was considered to be more important than a little witchcraft."

Lucy wondered if there also might have been more going on beneath the surface of the flower shop where she had worked. Scarlett selected her next cupcake. "My aunt and I are the only female witches in my family. It's hard because I've got four brothers, and there's all this male bravado about it, so I feel like I've got more to prove. Then last year, I was accepted to Ladywyck on a full scholarship because I created a variation of snapdragon that actually snaps." Scarlett held up her index finger to reveal that the tip was missing. "Creating flowers that are capable of rapid movement is considered a big accomplishment. Now, all the men in my family take me a little more seriously," Scarlett boasted. "But enough about me. When did you discover your talent for arranging flowers?"

Lucy didn't know how to answer that question. She still wasn't sure if she had any sort of talent for flowers. And certainly not a witch's "ability."

"Only recently. But I didn't know that Ladywyck had things like scholarships and degree programs. Daniel implied that the lodge wasn't very organized academically," Lucy said.

"Well, that's how he perceives it. But as I said the other day, Ladywyck serves different purposes for different people."

"So what purpose does it serve for him?" Lucy asked.

"He would say it's the food. You can usually find him hanging around the kitchen. But I think the lodge actually serves as a moral compass for him. I wasn't sure if you were aware that he's actually a Baddie."

"I kind of figured."

"He's what you would call a grifter witch. He came to Esther Wren trying to pass off Fool's Gold for real money." Scarlett leaned back in her chair and rubbed her stomach. "He was caught out pretty quickly. But instead of running him out of town, the guardians thought he could be of some use—teaching them the tricks of the trade, so to speak. They offered him a job and likely a ton of other incentives. He's now viewed as a traitor amongst his kind, but since he's the only male witch in town, he's a bit of a rock star. Girls really fall for his Fool's Gold routine."

"Yeah, he showed me."

"He did? When?" Scarlett's face flashed with jealousy.

"Last week. He took me on a tour of the lodge and showed me the attic. Helen caught us." Lucy paused. "He became a little weird after that."

"Weird? How so?"

"On the way home, he got quiet and moody."

"Baddies can only play nice for a while. Then they need to go home and have a timeout."

"You mean he's only pretending to be nice?"

"Not exactly. He has that side to him, and the closer he is to the lodge, the more it comes out. But the farther he gets away from it, the less effect the lodge has on him. Helen also seems to temper him. I just wish I had some kind of effect on him."

"So, you like him." Lucy smiled.

Scarlett sighed wistfully, then shrugged her shoulders. Lucy decided not to press any further. They finished their cupcakes and decided to take a walk through the downtown. As Scarlett talked about vegetation, fungi, and soil, Lucy contemplated potential talismans and energy sources. When they came to the public library, Lucy parted ways with Scarlett. She entered and made her way over to the designated "computer lounge," which was actually not much of a lounge, but rather a long table and three very well-worn computers. One was occupied by an old man playing solitaire, so Lucy sat at the one farthest from him.

"That one doesn't work," the man informed her. "It's been broken for almost six weeks and they're too cheap to fix it."

Lucy nodded. She got up and sat down at the one beside him.

"And that one has a sticky keyboard."

Lucy assumed he meant that the keys would stick when pressed, but in actuality, the keys were just sticky. Lucy touched one and recoiled in disgust. She took a tissue from her purse and tried to wipe the keyboard clean, but her efforts only seemed to make it worse. Very nimbly, she typed "Esther Wren Quill House" into the search bar and hit the Return key. At the top of the results list was the Ghost Charmers website. Lucy clicked on the link, dated two years ago, and a video popped up, blasting eerie music. She struggled to find the volume control as the old man looked over, visibly annoyed at the disturbance. Lucy muted the music and watched in silence as the very same redhead she'd seen with the van earlier in the day ran around the inside of her house with two other ghost charmers, scaring themselves to tears. At one point, they gathered in a candlelit circle in the living room and played wooden flutes—which Lucy took to be some sort of inane ghost-summoning ritual. At the end of the segment, the screen went black and an update was provided in dripping red font:

Unfortunately, we were unable to charm the spirits of
the Quill residence with our magical flutes.
The owners continued to experience many strange events,
including sightings of two children.
Personal items and furniture disappeared frequently.
The owners have since moved out.

Lucy drummed her fingers on the table and wondered if the hipster ghost charmer would ever be brave enough to add the latest footage of Millicent and Midgely's witch fight in front of her empty lot. Next to her, the old man blew his nose loudly into a handkerchief that he then placed on the table beside his computer. Suddenly, Lucy had a hunch as to why the keyboard was so sticky. She got up and went over to the front desk to use the hand sanitizer. Seeing her there, the librarian approached.

"Can I be of any assistance?" he asked.

"Actually, yes. I'm in sort of a strange predicament," Lucy said as she prepared to explain her situation.

"Yes, I know. Your house disappeared. I just saw it on the afternoon news—Channel 8 Syracuse." He motioned for her to come behind the front counter and quickly pushed aside a half-eaten tuna sandwich and juice box as he loaded up the news segment. Horrified, Lucy watched herself on the screen. She was pale and confused-looking, darting anxiously around her property like a trapped animal trying to escape the cheerful but predatory reporter. After interviewing several bystanders, the reporter concluded that the Quill House disappearance was likely the result of a practical joke.

"Doubtful," the librarian attested. "It's amazing the things they try to pass off in this town as practical jokes, hoaxes, elaborate pranks, and good old-fashioned tomfoolery. I would rather the world know the truth than think we're a bunch of idiots who live every day as if it were April Fool's Day."

"So why the cover-up?" Lucy asked.

The librarian's expression suddenly changed to worry, as if he wasn't really sure that this was a conversation he wanted to engage in, at least not out in the open. He leaned in close and spoke in a hushed voice. Lucy could smell the tinny scent of tuna fish on his breath.

"I think it's easier for *them*. I think those in charge would rather not have another Salem. You know—Halloweeny-type trinket shops and witch gawkers and God knows what else. I understand that, but I just wish they'd come up with a better explanation when, you know, *things go awry*." He shook his head. "Anyway, you said you needed some help?" he said, discreetly changing the topic.

"Oh, yes. Do you have any back issues of the *Esther Wren Gazette*?"

"Sure. I assume you'll want to start around 1973, 1974-ish? That's when the hauntings started at your house," the librarian explained. "I host a very discreet local ghost tour, so I know a little about your place."

"My house is on your ghost tour?"

The librarian smiled sheepishly.

"It is. And I have to admit, something doesn't add up. If the ghost really is Captain Quill, why did he hold off haunting it until 1974? I've always felt that there's another explanation. Of course, the disappearing act definitely adds another layer to the mystery. I'll meet you over by the microfiche reader," he said, pointing to a clunky machine with an oversized screen.

Lucy walked over to the device and reluctantly sat down. There was a panel of glass where a keyboard should be and a row of buttons beside the monitor that made little sense.

The librarian returned with several trays of film.

"It looks a little intimidating, but it's actually really easy to use," he said, turning the machine on and inserting a sheet of film. There was a dial on the right-hand side that he rotated until the image came into focus. After giving Lucy a brief lesson on how to change the sheets and how to print, he proceeded to stand behind her, peering over her shoulder for several minutes until a family needed his assistance in checking out their books.

An hour passed as Lucy sifted through various articles about fall fairs and influenza outbreaks, but it was the word *hellcat* that stopped her in her tracks. Lucy adjusted the focus on a front-page article from August 20, 1973, with the attention-grabbing headline "Hellcat Eviction Turns Violent" and instantly recalled Eugenia's mysterious warning at the Potluck Pottery Social. Underneath the headline was a grainy black-and-white photo of a woman with long frizzy hair, wearing bell-bottom jeans and a fringe vest, being tackled to the ground by three police officers. She was doubled over, her face looking toward the camera—eyes angry slits, and mouth frozen in mid-scream. Lucy accidentally hit the zoom dial and the image suddenly magnified, offering an up-close view of the black pit of the woman's open mouth. Lucy reared back, but as she struggled to adjust the focus again, she caught sight of something familiar in the distant background: her house.

The article reported that on August 19, 1973, Helva Jane (a.k.a. the Hellcat), a resident of Esther Wren, was forcibly evicted from the house she was renting. The article referred to her residence as a flophouse with an open-door policy for vagrants and drug addicts. After a litany of complaints from neighbors and the landlord, the police were able to evict the tenant on account of health code violations. Several animals were removed from the premises as well, including cats, raccoons, squirrels, rats, bats, and several birds. Near the end, the article mentioned that Helva Jane was a known menace to Esther Wren; she had a long history of run-ins with the law that involved shoplifting, assault, and arson, to name a few. Lucy printed a copy of the article and then returned to the sticky computer, where she ran an internet search on Helva Jane. Somewhere around 1999, the results suggested, the Hellcat had disappeared from Esther Wren altogether. She was last seen at Adams Grocery, stealing firewood from the parking lot. In 2002 someone set up a fan site called "Finding Helva Jane." It had a sizable following, with numerous Hellcat sightings reported throughout North America.

Who was this terrible person? Lucy wondered. The fan site provided little information as to her background, or why she had amassed over five thousand followers. There was only one other photo: it showed Helva Jane standing on the sagging porch of a ramshackle old farmhouse. She was almost unrecognizable in her groomed state, dressed in a navy kimono embroidered with a dragon, her wavy hair combed and hanging to her waist. She appeared regal but reclusive; her back was to the viewer, but her head was tilted just enough to reveal that her left eye was watching the camera. There were five other people on the porch: three women and two men, one of whom faintly resembled a much younger Lyle from the hardware store. The women were particularly unusual-looking: tall and willowy with high, hollow cheekbones and dressed in loose-fitting gunnysack dresses. Their eyes were dreamy but their mouths were mean—like beautiful savages. They stood in front of the two men, positioned almost protectively as they held up various animal pelts, like hunters proudly showing off their kill.

Lucy scrolled down to a thread of comments. Black Raven wrote: "Helva Jane is Legend. Thought I saw her and her followers peddling bone necklaces in Venice Beach, California, 2004." Pale Luke wrote: "Helva Jane is the force that dances among us." TexasMatt wrote: "She lives in the woods just outside Brimstone, Ontario." Vinegar Tom wrote: "She's my aunt and I see her every Christmas." Lucy printed off as much as she could from the website and stuffed the pages into her purse. Although none of it made much sense to her yet, Lucy felt that she was finally on the right track.

The librarian stood up and announced that the library was closing in five minutes. He approached Lucy and asked if she'd had any luck. She responded wordlessly with a nod. Then she grabbed her purse and her shopping bag and headed out the door.

CHAPTER ELEVEN

Houses

Lucy took the long route home from the library. She was in no real hurry to sit the evening away in a borrowed chair and be pitied like an unfortunate lawn ornament by those whose homes didn't vanish into thin air. She was also certain that the volume of dog walkers and car gawkers would likely increase thanks to the news feature, but she hadn't quite prepared herself for the scene that greeted her when she turned onto her street. At least five hundred people covered the road, sidewalks, and front lawns. They had brought lawn chairs and blankets; some had even pitched small tents on neighboring properties. Two more ghost hunter trucks had arrived, alongside a handful of food trucks that were busy serving up cheesy fries and funnel cakes to the hungry masses. The Channel 8 news truck had returned with Julie Blue, who was now conducting an interview with the hipster ghost charmer and his magical flute. As Lucy hurried across the street she saw two young girls sitting cross-legged on the grass. They were singing and clapping their hands together.

Lucy Crisp, Lucy Crisp
Oh where has your house gone?
Up up up in the air
or fallen deep underground.
(clap clap
clap clap clap)

Poor, poor Lucy Crisp,
With hair like hot cross buns.
Where will you go, where will you go
It seems you have nowhere to run.
(clap clap
clap clap clap)

Lucy Crisp, Lucy Crisp
Now you must sit and wait.
You must hope and must pray
that your house will return one day.
(clap clap
clap clap clap)

Lucy reached up and felt her braid, suddenly self-conscious. Did it really look like a breakfast food? A group of teenagers recognized her and began to take pictures. She quickly changed direction and walked until she reached the raggedy yellow grass that lined her front pathway. Her homeless hamper was now overflowing with canned goods and clothing, and a folding table had been set up beside the hamper, displaying an array of various casseroles and baked goods. There were also bouquets of flowers, condolence cards, and teddy bears with sympathy balloons piled up along the sidewalk. Over by the lilac tree, a vigil was in session consisting of three women and three men sitting in a candlelit circle, holding hands and praying.

Lucy went to check on the rabbits and when she returned she saw Helen and Daniel standing in the middle of her property. They looked dazed and concerned by all the activity.

"Lucy, we would like to offer you our heartfelt condolences." Helen stepped forward, took Lucy's hand, and held it gently in her own.

"Thank you," Lucy replied, choked up by Helen's sympathy.

"I have a room at the lodge that I would like to offer you until your house reappears. It overlooks the vineyard and it has a lovely four-poster bed. There's actually a little staircase that you have to use to get into it—it's absolutely darling."

It was the most tempting proposition she had been given to date, so tempting, in fact, that Lucy even surprised herself when she declined the offer.

"I really appreciate it, but I would rather stay here. You know, to keep an eye on everything."

"Of course. I totally understand. But if you need anything, or change your mind, please let me know."

"Actually, I do have a question."

Helen nodded in anticipation while a distracted Daniel waved at a group of pretty brown-haired girls.

"Who is Helva Jane?" Lucy asked.

Daniel's attention suddenly returned to Lucy.

"Why do you want to know about her?" he asked.

"She lived in my house back in the seventies, and I'm pretty certain she's behind all this."

Daniel seemed surprised.

Lucy looked over at Helen, who appeared to be thinking deeply.

"Yes, she did. I had forgotten. Almost forty years ago. The town evicted her. It made the papers," Helen said.

"Do you know what became of her?" Lucy asked.

"I'm not really sure," Helen responded. "I haven't heard about her in years. My understanding is that she left town."

"Was she dangerous?"

Helen and Daniel shared a glance. Helen leaned in toward Lucy.

"Well, I didn't know Helva Jane personally, so I can't say for certain just what her motives were, but she was undisciplined—some may even say wild. There are certain rules we follow and she was, well, a deviant. She wrote a book about twenty years ago that catapulted her to stardom amongst a certain segment of society."

"What was the book about?" Lucy asked.

"It involved some aspects of darker magic," Daniel explained.

"Like hexes and curses?"

Helen nodded. "Something along those lines. I don't expect many copies were printed, but I can ask some of my sources if they can acquire a copy, if you feel it would help you with your house."

"I would really appreciate that."

"Of course," Helen replied.

A young boy holding a sparkler darted between them. Night had fallen, and the crowd was beginning to thin. Those who remained appeared to be settling in for the evening, clustering around portable barbecues roasting hot dogs and marshmallows. Daniel went off to talk to the group of brunettes, and Helen bid Lucy good night and disappeared into the crowd. Lucy wandered aimlessly for a while, soaking in the festive atmosphere while doing her best to remain incognito. The air smelled of burnt sugar and grease, triggering her appetite once again. She found a secluded spot near the end of her street, and while perched on the edge of a curb, she ate a dinner that consisted of a bean burrito and a funnel cake topped with powdered sugar, whipped cream, and candied strawberries. Afterward, she listened to the town troubadour, who sang a more melodic version of the song that the two young girls had been singing earlier. She was relieved that he had changed the verse "hair like hot cross buns" to the more poetic "hair like a wreath of roses." When he finished his set, Lucy realized that the temperature had dropped considerably. The thought of sleeping another night in the greenhouse was unthinkable, especially after being tempted by the four-poster bed. She yearned for privacy and comfort. Someplace quiet but close, where she could think about the day's findings. Lucy discreetly slipped into Brenda's back garden and retrieved the keys from under the flowerpot. It would just be for the night, and she would never have to know.

Brenda's house was calm and quiet: an ideal refuge from the chaos outside. It was decorated in a mishmash of shabby chic and 1960s modern: white-painted furniture mixed with funky mustard-colored lamps and teak chairs, likely all rummaged from thrift shops and yard sales. Lucy felt a twinge of jealousy at how Brenda had managed to make such an inviting home from so little. It was something she had yet to accomplish with her own home—although she did have a few more obstacles in her way than Brenda. Lucy wandered around the kitchen and living room surveying the similarities between her home and Brenda's, appreciating the same quality of workmanship. But whereas her house was grand, Brenda's was cozy.

She entered the living room and admired Brenda's carefully curated collection of vintage still-life paintings displayed over the sofa. All tea roses in different shades of pink, cream, and yellow. On the opposite wall, above the fireplace, was another group of paint- ings—all portraits: a woman with rhinestone cat-eye glasses, a pen- sive man in a gray suit holding a pipe, a redhead wearing a peasant blouse and a crown of dandelions, and, at the bottom right-hand corner, a portrait of a young boy with a monocle that Lucy found a little off-putting. She looked around to make sure that there were no enchanted portraits of Persian kittens, and then she sat down on Brenda's lumpy sofa and pulled the picture of Helva Jane and her followers from her purse. A chill shot down her spine at the possibil- ity of those hollow-cheeked women stalking her, circling her house while she slept, creeping through her dark halls, touching her belong- ings and moving furniture around. She tucked the picture back into her purse, rubbed her eyes, and lay back on the sofa. Sleep needed little encouragement, and she drifted off instantly.

Lucy woke up the next morning feeling rested but a little disoriented from sleeping yet another night in unfamiliar surroundings. She turned on her phone and checked the lengthy string of texts from her father, repeatedly asking her to call him. He made no mention of seeing her on the news, but she knew it would only be a matter of time before his attention shifted from the arts section of his newspaper into the actual news section. She texted back "Everything is good!" hoping it would buy her another day of sleuthing.

In bare feet and a wrinkled dress, Lucy shuffled into Brenda's kitchen and looked around for coffee but found only a coffee canister filled with teabags. It would have to do. While the kettle was heating, she went in search of the bathroom. At the back of the cottage, there were three doors, all shut. Lucy opened the first one to find Brenda's bedroom. It was bright and tidy, with faded lilac wallpaper and a queen bed with a white-wicker peacock headboard. Over by the window was a little sewing corner with a sewing machine and several shelves filled with stacks of folded fabric, thread, and patterns. Feeling guilty for invading Brenda's privacy, Lucy was about to shut the door when a piece of fabric caught her eye. It sat on top of a pile of discarded remnants and crumpled sewing paper. Lucy could see little dots of orange that resembled carrots. As Lucy slowly approached the sewing table, she grew more and more certain that it was the very same bunny rabbit fabric that had tormented her all summer long. But it wasn't until she was actually holding it in her hands, massaging the thin cotton material between her fingertips, that she knew beyond a shadow of a doubt: it was definitely the same. In that moment, Lucy felt unsteady. She sat down on the edge of Brenda's bed, gripping the bunny fabric tightly in her sweaty hands.

Lucy's mind raced back through her previous conversations with Brenda. From the very beginning, Lucy had sensed resentment from

Brenda over the fact that Lucy had been able to afford the bigger house, not to mention that the place had also been Brenda's ancestral home. Could the disturbances all be part of an elaborate scheme to devalue the house until Brenda could afford to buy it? Could she be in on it with Millicent, Helva Jane, and the Trumbo brothers? Lucy imagined all of them holed up in a warehouse on the outskirts of town with all the pieces of her disassembled house—waiting until she had been sufficiently spooked.

The sound of a screaming kettle snapped Lucy back to reality. She leapt to her feet and smoothed out the chenille bedspread, set the fabric back down where she had found it, and hurried back to the kitchen to turn the burner off. Having lost all interest in the tea, Lucy headed back down the hallway and opened the door opposite Brenda's to discover a cheerful sunlit room with periwinkle-blue wallpaper patterned with tall ships. Like Brenda's room, Marigold's was extremely tidy: toys and books neatly stacked and put away. Even her porcelain doll collection looked pristine and untouched—their dresses and bonnets all perfectly arranged. The only signs of play were the crayon drawings scattered across Marigold's desk.

Mostly, they were scribbles of polka-dotted rabbits and slanted houses with curls of smoke swirling from chimneys. Lucy noticed that one of the drawings was stuck to the edge of a bottle of cough syrup. As she struggled to free it without tearing the page, the bottle tipped over and bright pink cough syrup pooled out onto the desk. The scent of medicine and strawberries filled the air, reminding her of the cloyingly sweet smell that had permeated her living room the morning of the windstorm.

A feeling of unease began to grow in the pit of her stomach. She searched around for something she could use to wipe up the syrup and noticed a package of tissues, beside a shoebox, sitting on a bookcase. The box was battered and bent, and the lid sat slightly askew. Lucy gently picked up the box, and a tiny cake tumbled out and landed on the carpet. It was about the size of a nickel, made of plastic, five layers high, with painted white cream oozing out between each layer, and crowned with a ring of red cherries. The little hairs on the back of Lucy's neck stood on end when she realized it was a miniature copy of the Black Forest cake that had magically appeared in her kitchen during her father's visit. Curious, Lucy set the box down on the desk, removed the lid, and peered inside. At first all she could see was a tangle of tiny limbs. Then, a piece of pale-blue denim caught her attention; she reached into the box and pulled out a small doll, the length of her hand, of a man clothed in a denim pantsuit—a size too small, with two large pockets crudely stitched on the front of the jacket. She gasped and dropped the doll. Her body felt tingly and her heart raced as she tried to understand how Marigold had come to be in possession of a doll that so closely resembled the man who had appeared in Lucy's kitchen. Lucy peered into the box again and saw another doll: a woman wearing red high-heeled shoes—identical to the pair that had appeared on her staircase the morning of the electrical storm. She rummaged deeper into the box and pulled out the dolls of a red-haired boy, a blonde girl with freckles, a butler with heavy black brows, a maid, and a Siamese cat with turquoise eyes—the color of swimming pools.

"Mr. Mews?" Lucy said, almost choking on her words.

As she turned away from the box, trying to collect her thoughts, she noticed that one of the louvered closet doors was open and there was something large and square, draped in an old cotton sheet, sitting against the back wall of the closet. Lucy's palms began to sweat, and her skin prickled with anticipation as she crouched down and lifted the corner of the sheet. She saw what appeared to be a porch column, painted white, with delicate gingerbread brackets—an exact replica of her own porch column—and she immediately recalled Eugenia's statement from the Potluck Pottery Social: "It too has such a lovely porch."

Lucy stood up and in one swooping gesture yanked the sheet off. The room immediately fell into shadow. Something had altered—something massive had shifted—but she didn't know exactly what. Then, her vision slanted, and she felt the sensation of being inside a rapidly descending elevator. The floor came at her fast, her legs buckling beneath her, and she hit the ground hard. She lay on the carpet, dazed and dizzy, on the brink of blackness, but the sudden burst of muffled screams and car horns outside lured her back. She sat up and looked out the window—where she immediately saw what had cast the shadow. Her house had returned. She looked back at the dollhouse and realized that it was an immaculate reproduction of her own house. And in that moment, Lucy understood: she had found the talisman.

The dollhouse was old but in good condition, and it was sparsely decorated with the same motley assortment of furnishings as her own house—only on a miniature scale. Mostly, they were secondhand pieces, but there had been some improvisation with a few items, like the tattered blue washcloth that served as the living room carpet and the infamous bunny chair. Lucy reached in, picked the chair up, and cradled it in the palm of her hand. It looked as if it had once been a wooden chair, padded with cotton balls and then slipcovered and stapled at the seams. Even in its tiny state, the chair still gave Lucy goose bumps. Next to it was a few droplets of something red—still fresh and sticky. Lucy leaned in closer and smelled the scent of strawberry-flavored cough syrup.

On a hunch, Lucy picked up the sheet and draped it back over the dollhouse. The room filled with light. She looked out the window to see that her house had vanished once again. She pulled the sheet off, and within the blink of an eye, her house reappeared and the room fell into shadow. Lucy repeated this action several times, driving the crowd outside into hysterics. Then she went over to the shoebox and fetched Mr. Mews; she placed him gently on the bunny chair, where he belonged.

The dollhouse was heavy and awkward, but Lucy managed to carry it across her lawn and up the front steps as the crowd buzzed around her. She hesitated before entering her house, wondering if she should address her audience or possibly make some sort of speech. Instead she just held up the dollhouse, hoping they might understand the significance of it. The gesture was met with a mass of confused faces gazing back at her. She lowered the dollhouse and went inside.

Mr. Mews greeted Lucy in the front foyer with loud purrs that encouraged plenty of chin scratching. After she hugged and fed him,

Lucy made a few phone calls. Helen and Daniel were the first to arrive. At first they studied the dollhouse only visibly—peeking into each room as Daniel admired the workmanship and pointed out impressive details, like the carvings on the staircase, noting how perfectly they matched the woodwork in Lucy's house. Helen continued her examination in silence, until she stopped abruptly. Her fingers slid down the chimney of the dollhouse and wriggled around until she pulled out a tiny piece of paper, tightly rolled into a shape that resembled a cigarette.

"I believe I have found it," Helen announced.

Suddenly, Lucy's dining room fireplace groaned and shook, and then a great billow of black smoke blanketed the floor with soot and dead leaves. Lucy could have sworn she heard something that sounded like laughter. It was low and guttural, but female, and it quickly faded away. Daniel and Helen choked and coughed while Lucy ran around and opened the windows and the front door in an attempt to clear the air.

"My apologies for the intrusion, but the front door was wide open."

Emerald Parker stood in the front hall, looking flawless in a seventies-style ice-blue pantsuit.

"We found the talisman!" Lucy exclaimed.

Emerald surveyed the mess in the living room and tiptoed around the leaf piles until her eyes came to rest upon the dollhouse.

"Of course," Emerald said as she circled it cautiously. "This makes perfect sense."

Helen handed the tightly rolled piece of paper over to Emerald, who gently unwound it.

"This is Helva Jane's work," Emerald announced.

"How do you know? What does it say?" Lucy asked.

"It's a symbol—essentially a spell. But Helva's initial is at the bottom. It's also dated August 18, 1973."

"Is it normal to date a spell?" Lucy asked.

"It's not unheard of. Like milk, spells expire, and some witches like to see how long they can last. Obviously this one had some real staying power."

"August 18 was the day before she was evicted," Lucy said.

"Where did you find the dollhouse?" Emerald asked.

"It was at Brenda Merriweather's—my next-door neighbor. Her ancestor Captain Quill built both of our houses, and I suspect he made the dollhouse too. When I bought the house, Millicent Brown told me that Captain Quill made children's toys," Lucy said as she pointed to his portrait over the fireplace. "I found it in her daughter's bedroom. They're on vacation right now, and I was checking the house for them when I discovered it," Lucy said, feeling a little guilty about stretching the truth. "I found it under a sheet in her daughter's bedroom, and when I removed the sheet, my house reappeared. There was also a shoebox full of dollhouse figurines and furnishings, all things that have appeared in this house—including my cat," Lucy said as she looked over to see that Mr. Mews was now sleeping soundly in the bunny chair. "Do you think they were doing all of this on purpose?" Lucy asked Emerald.

Emerald shook her head from side to side. "I don't get any sense of that. I would imagine that when her daughter was playing with the dollhouse, she was unknowingly working the hex—like a puppeteer of sorts. You see, part of Helva Jane's genius was the simplicity of her work. Many witches tend to get bogged down in the details, and it can suffocate a spell. The one on your house is so basic. Literally translated, it says: 'Give this house life.'"

Helen went over to the window and looked outside. The French Braids were gathered on their front porch, busy examining the contents of their canning jars.

"I didn't quite realize that they had advanced so far," Helen said to Daniel. "Although I suppose I should have, given how strange the weather has been this summer."

"Well, the oldest one has to be getting close to sixteen," Daniel added. "And didn't she get into some sort of scuffle with Millicent the other morning?"

Helen nodded. "Yes, I heard that too. And I heard she won. At least, according to Norma Adams at the grocery store. It was all the talk in the checkout line."

"She did. I saw everything. She blew her around the street like a kite," Lucy stated.

"I would have paid money to see that!" Daniel threw his head back and laughed, then stopped abruptly when he caught a stern look from Helen.

"Those are storm jars, right? Like the ones you have in the curiosities room?" Lucy asked.

Helen shot another stern look at Daniel.

"Yes, they're storm jars," Helen said. "It's how weather witches are trained." Helen paused. "Do you know what a weather witch is? Or did Daniel neglect to explain the different varieties of witches to you during your secret attic education?"

Lucy looked down at her feet. "I assume they can control the weather?"

"Yes. And not only the weather; they can manipulate water as well. You see, weather witches are direct descendants of sea witches. The first witches. They are rare and very powerful. Obviously, having potentially four in one town is a concern. In each jar they've manifested a different type of storm. An electric storm, a hurricane, some jars can even hold tiny tornados. Their grandmother, Agnes Drummond, made wonderfully elaborate storm jars and sold them at the farmer's market many moons ago."

"Lucy, can you recall when most of the disturbances occurred? Was it rainy or possibly windy?" Emerald asked.

"Yes, every time."

"Well, I think I now know why the spell became so powerful—it was feeding off the Drummond girls," Emerald said. "I'm fairly certain the spell would have withered and died, had it not been for them."

Everyone grew quiet and stared out at the four young girls who were now lying on their lawn dreamily staring up at the cloudless sky.

"So, what do I do now? If we break the spell, what will happen to Mr. Mews?" Lucy asked. "I've grown really attached to him."

"Of course you have. I think the best course of action would be for us to take the spell back to the lodge and speak with a few of our members about how to properly dispose of it without harming your cat. At the very least, I'm sure there's a way we can modify it," Helen said as she gave Lucy a hug good-bye.

Lucy walked them to the front porch and saw that the crowd outside had swelled once again. There were now several people

standing on Brenda's lawn, trampling all over her lavender, attempting to get a good angle for their selfies. Lucy was about to shut the door when she saw her father walking up the front path.

"What is going on?" he said, a bewildered expression on his face. He paused to look back at the crowd. "Is there a parade or something?"

"Dad, we need to talk. You'd better come inside."

―――

Brenda and Marigold returned home from their vacation a week later. At first, Brenda seemed more concerned about her trampled lavender than she was to hear about Lucy's break-and-enter and the discovery of the dollhouse. But once Brenda put Marigold to bed, she joined Lucy on her porch for a glass of lemonade.

"I didn't grow up here. I grew up in Fountainview, which is two hours away, so I was kept pretty sheltered from the events of this town—at least initially," Brenda explained. "But in the summers, I would often stay with my grandparents for a few weeks, and I can remember overhearing things, you know, about that Hellcat woman. Of course, nothing was ever said outright until one visit when my grandmother enrolled me in a day camp and these two girls kept teasing me about how my grandparents had once owned the 'Hellcat House.' They said that a witch called the Hellcat had lived there with her followers and performed séances and black magic rituals until she was kicked out. They said that she left behind an evil so powerful that the house had become infected with it. When I questioned my grandfather, his reply was that the only thing that ever haunted that house was Captain Quill. He often made up these dramatically silly ghost stories about him, which I think is what the house became more known for."

"I suppose he was just trying to protect you from all that unpleasantness. People probably wanted to forget about Helva Jane and replace those stories with something a little less sinister."

"I found the dollhouse at the annual library rummage sale a couple of years ago and immediately knew that my great-uncle had made it, so I bought it for Marigold. I had heard from my grandparents that there was a dollhouse, but it had gone missing years ago. The only thing that was a little weird about it was how often the furniture would disappear. In fact, a few months back, I woke up to discover that almost all the furniture was missing, and the portrait of Captain Quill that normally hung above the fireplace was in the attic."

Lucy bit down on her lip. "That was me. I sent a bunch of things off to auction and I put him in the attic."

"Oh." A look of guilt washed over Brenda's face. "I thought it was Marigold. This year, she's been all about flushing things down the toilet. I spent the summer scavenging yard sales and the internet for dollhouse furniture. I even made a few of my own things, like the curtains and a chair that I reupholstered with some fabric left over from Marigold's sundresses."

"Yes, that was very creative of you." Lucy hesitated as she struggled to find the right words. "My cat has really taken to it."

"I had a funny feeling that something was off the morning we left—almost like I'd forgotten something, which I just assumed was because of the rabbits. It was a busy morning, with tidying up, putting Marigold's toys away. There's nothing worse than coming home from a vacation to a messy house. When I was vacuuming, I moved the dollhouse into the closet and covered it with an old sheet. We left very early in the morning, so I guess I just didn't notice your house missing in the dark."

The final piece of the puzzle locked into place: Lucy's house had disappeared because Brenda was a neat freak.

Their conversation was interrupted by a young couple strolling along the sidewalk. The two were attempting to be subtle, but Lucy could tell by their overly casual behavior that they were really there to take a look at the house. Possibly even snap a photo or two.

"I think you'll be getting that for quite a while," Brenda said as she waved at the couple, who seemed more than a little embarrassed as they returned the wave. "But at least with school starting soon you'll likely be too busy to notice. Are you getting excited?"

Lucy was eager to spend more time at the lodge, but she had yet to conjure up the same level of enthusiasm for her program.

"To be honest, that typewriter has made me rethink things."

"What typewriter?" Brenda asked.

"The old black one that was sitting on the front porch when I moved in. I assumed it was from the dollhouse."

"I've never seen a typewriter in the dollhouse," Brenda replied.

A lone woman with a fluffy white dog approached the house. She stopped when she saw Brenda and Lucy.

"Are you the girl who lives here?" She pointed at Lucy.

Lucy took in a deep breath and nodded.

"You should sue the town, you know. They're well aware of the problems with this house," the woman shouted.

Lucy nodded politely, trying not to engage with the stranger any further.

"It's ridiculous the things they make us tolerate. If I were mayor, I would run every last one of those darn witches out. They're destroying our town, you know."

An awkward silence fell upon them as they all watched the woman's dog sniff around Lucy's lawn before it finally lifted its leg and peed on her white picket fence.

"Good boy, Rochester," the woman praised the dog as they walked away.

CHAPTER TWELVE

Bees

The day before the fall semester began, Lucy was called into Helen's office.

"Please excuse the mess. We're getting ready for the annual fall fair," Helen explained, pointing to several crates surrounding her desk that were piled high with jams, honey, and pickles. "There's just so much inventory to organize. Fortunately, it looks like this year we will finally have enough of our Blackbird Jam. It's a top seller." Helen picked up a jar and handed it to Lucy. "For your father. I know he's a foodie. Don't worry, it doesn't contain any blackbirds—they just forage the fruit for us." Helen gestured toward an alcove furnished with a burgundy loveseat and matching wingback chairs. "Please take a seat."

Lucy sat down in one of the chairs and noticed several bees buzzing around the room, feeding from the many flower arrangements decorating Helen's office.

"Excuse the bees," Helen said. "It's that time of year, and we never like to interfere with their work. They just love my hydrangeas."

"Oh, I don't mind bees," Lucy replied.

"Wonderful." Helen took the seat opposite Lucy. "So, I understand that the enchantment on your house was altered successfully without harming your cat. Any changes in his behavior?"

"Not really. He still sleeps a lot, but at least he doesn't disappear anymore."

"And how about you? Have you and your father recovered from all the excitement yet?"

"I think so. My dad finally went back to the city a few days ago. But I don't think he will ever accept what actually happened. His latest theory is faulty wiring."

"But he must be happy that you found a housemate. I understand she's a student here."

Lucy nodded. "She's majoring in cursed and enchanted objects, so she's really happy about living in a house that was at the center of so much paranormal activity," Lucy said while she watched the fattest bee she had ever seen disappear inside the trumpet of a daffodil. "I didn't know daffodils were still in season."

"Daffodils are always in season here." Helen smiled. "And while we're on the subject of daffodils, do you know what they symbolize?"

"Spring?" Lucy suggested.

"Close. Daffodils symbolize new beginnings—which is essentially why you're here."

Lucy took a deep breath, knowing that this was her opportunity to broach the subject of changing programs.

"About that. I've been meaning to talk with you about something. I'm not sure if the floral artistry program is where I'm supposed to be."

Helen raised her eyebrows and leaned in a little closer.

"Don't get me wrong—I love flowers, but I'm not sure if that's where my strength lies. I was wondering if you had any space left in your creative writing program. I know it's late, and the program is probably—"

"Does that mean you got some use out of the typewriter?"

Lucy paused. "That was you?"

Helen nodded.

"But how did you know that I liked to write?"

"The essay that you submitted alongside your portfolio. The flower arranging was competent but writing is your gift. Whoopsie Daisy?" Helen laughed and clapped her hands together. "You had me in stitches with your description of your dog-walking duties. But my question is, Why have you been avoiding pursuing writing as a career? It comes so naturally to you."

Lucy thought for a moment.

"Fear, I guess. Fear of failing at something that I really like. Plus, I don't think my father wants me to follow in his footsteps. He struggled quite a bit early on."

"Hardship and struggle is what makes us strong. It makes us interesting. It gives our lives a plot. Think about your essay. How dull would it have been if you had described a perfect life? And not only that, it would have been dishonest." Helen paused. "It's natural to feel adrift sometimes, and it's during those times that we become vulnerable to other people's influences—however well-meaning they might be. But if you trust your instincts, you will eventually get to where you need to be. Just look at our worker bee friends here. These ladies follow their intuition and survive. And not only do they survive, but they create something extraordinary as well," Helen said, pointing to a jar of honey sitting on her desk. "To be honest, we knew that this summer was going to present a challenge to you—we could tell by your chart."

"My chart?"

"Of course. We create charts for all of our students who are under serious consideration. It's based a little on your astrological sign, date of birth, and a few more relevant factors. We like to make sure that our students are meant to be here."

"And I'm meant to be here?"

Helen nodded. "Just not in the floral artistry program."

"But why didn't you tell me sooner?"

"It wasn't our place to tell you. We don't mind subtle suggestion—hence the typewriter—but you needed to come to that decision on your own. Which you did, and with one day to spare."

Helen handed Lucy a key with a yellow tassel and a pair of white cotton gloves.

"Welcome to the creative writing program. The key is for your writing cabin, number twelve, located at the top of the hill, and your timetable and course curriculum are waiting for you in the registry office. The gloves are for the Room of Curiosities. Given what you've experienced over the summer, we've also decided to grant you full membership, which means you will have access to all of the restricted rooms in the lodge. I predict that the attic will be a great source of inspiration for you."

Lucy slid her hands into the cotton gloves before picking up the storm jar and holding it toward the window—hoping that the light would help to reveal its contents—but the fog was too dense. The label on the jar read *San Francisco Bay, 1989,* and it was the fifth storm jar Lucy had discovered in the Room of Curiosities. Almost every item she had uncovered over the past few weeks had an incredible story bound to it. She felt a sense of sympathy for the enchantments—locked away in a dingy attic capturing cobwebs when they should have been capturing imaginations. Lucy felt a little like the hippie witch that Daniel had described, but instead of possessing the necessary magical skills to release the enchantments from their confinement, she would have to settle for telling their stories instead. But where to begin? There was an album filled with old photographs of young children gleefully holding miniature horses in the palms of their hands, and a bookshelf lined with model ships in bottles that rocked and swayed against invisible waves. In the far corner of the attic was a cupboard stacked with jars of unmeltable snow neatly labeled and dated like preserves. Lucy had even stumbled upon a cavernous seashell that still smelled of brine and seaweed, and if you listened very carefully, you could hear mermaids' whispers. There was one item in particular that ignited Lucy's curiosity. It was called the Smoking Fur Stole, and pinned to the hem of garment was a letter about its owner:

THE SMOKING FUR STOLE

Opal Brown (1881–1927) was a wealthy businesswoman and restaurateur, most known for her nightclub The Opal, located in Lower Manhattan during the roaring twenties that magically evaded the strictures of prohibition. The Opal was lavishly decorated with opulent furnishings and artifacts from Miss Brown's exotic travels—most famously a taxidermied polar bear that greeted guests at the front entrance.

It was well known amongst a certain segment of New York society that Opal Brown had a strong aptitude for magic and an even stronger head for business, but she had never been particularly lucky at love. At the age of forty-five, her luck seemed to take a turn for the better when she met a thirty-four-year-old Argentinian play-boy, Javier Rule, while traveling abroad. By all accounts, the couple was very happy in spite of their age difference and spent the next year cutting a swath through New York society. But their love affair was strained when rumors started to circulate that Javier had an appetite for gambling and an even stronger appetite for pretty, young blondes.

On the evening of April 7, 1927, Opal Brown returned home to New York a day early from a buying trip in Egypt and made an unscheduled stop at her restaurant to check the books.

Unbeknownst to Opal Brown, her fiancé was dining with Willow Douglas, a striking doe-eyed nightclub singer with whom Javier was rumored to be having an affair. They had spent the evening canoodling by candle-light and drinking Canadian whiskey when suddenly they

discovered that they were being watched: Opal Brown stood silently, not quite five feet away.

Witness accounts vary as to what exactly happened next: some claim that the room began to shake, causing all the liquor bottles to fall from the bar shelves; others say that, one by one, the liquor bottles exploded. Whatever the cause, within seconds, the alcohol caught fire and the room became a raging inferno. Opal Brown perished in the fire along with Javier Rule, Willow Douglas, and thirty-three restaurant patrons. Only one item was found completely intact: the fur stole that Opal Brown had been wearing that night.

Lucy leaned in closer to the stole and caught a faint whiff of smoke. "Knock knock!" A cheery voice broke Lucy's focus, and she looked up to see Scarlett standing in the doorway holding a tray with a silver teapot. "I hope I'm not disturbing you, but Helen said that you were up here. I brought you some vanilla tea and lavender shortbread."

"Oh, that's so nice of you." Lucy stood up and cleared a spot by her laptop, and Scarlett set the tray down.

"The lavender is a new variety that I created. It has a slightly different flavor than what you are probably used to—a little more minty. Which is an improvement over the previous strain, which smelled like farm animals."

"Well, I'm relieved to hear you improved it. Can you stay for a cup?" Lucy asked.

"I would love to, but I'm filling in for Mademoiselle de Havilland—she mishandled some poison ivy in her last flower-pressing class—and I'm not exactly prepared. Big turnout expected. It's Flower Pressing 101 for senior citizens. They're being bused in from the Shady Lane Retirement Home."

"What flower are you pressing today?"

"Queen Anne's lace, but my batch is looking kind of mangy and I don't think it's going to press very nicely. I think it's because of that heat wave we had a while back—what a weird summer it was." Suddenly Scarlett's eyes grew wide. "Did you hear that the Drummond sisters are being tutored here after school?"

Lucy hadn't heard, but she had noticed the French Braids' absence from their front porch for the past several weeks.

"Helen called in a global warming expert who has been training them to use their skills more productively—you know, with climate change. I've heard that they've really taken to it. I think they like all the attention they're getting." Scarlett glanced around the room. "How can you stand being up here? It's so hot, and it smells like old things. Half of this stuff is probably infested with gnats."

"I suppose it's the price I have to pay for inspiration," Lucy said as she pinned the letter back on the stole.

"Are you going to write about that stole?" Scarlett asked warily. "It gives me the creeps."

"Well, not the stole exactly, but the story behind it is pretty interesting."

"Didn't it belong to Millicent Brown?"

"No, but it did belong to an ancestor of hers."

"Well, you're a braver person than I am. Anything to do with that woman scares the life out of me." She gave Lucy a quick hug and headed off to prepare for class.

Lucy picked up a piece of shortbread and nibbled the edge while gazing out the window. She saw Eugenia Forrester trampling through the south-side gardens with a small group of people trailing behind her, all wearing identical green rubber boots. Suddenly, Eugenia came to an abrupt stop and pulled a large toadstool from the earth. Lucy realized that it was Eugenia's Finding Fairies class, in which she led a group of like-minded fairy followers through the gardens, digging up vegetation in search of the hidden fairy world. The class was a controversial topic amongst the members of the lodge, as it involved an absurd amount of destruction to the gardens and lawns, but it was being temporarily tolerated due to Eugenia's sizable donations to the upkeep and improvement of Ladywyck Lodge for the past twenty years.

As Lucy sat down and poured herself a cup of tea, the room suddenly brightened. She looked out the window again and saw that the sun had cut through the clouds and lit up the garden. A silvery mist enveloped Eugenia, making her appear otherworldly—like a fairy herself. Lucy smiled while easing back into her chair, and as she cradled her cup of tea, she wondered what possible harm there could be in writing about the eccentric antics of these wonderfully magical people? Then she took a sip of tea and burnt her tongue.

The Courting of the
Common Garden Fair

Eugenia Gilliland-Forrester

VICTORY TO AGNES BAKERY, NEW YORK CITY
by Astrid Vultrin, August 30, 2014

While attending an exclusive launch party for a friend's organic salad dressing line (to be covered next week), I stumbled upon something miraculous. As we crowded into communal tables in the back garden of his Greenwich apartment, I encountered a dinner roll that truly took my breath away. I don't usually bother with the bread basket. But that night, probably due to the shortage of carbs, I elected to take one. Even before it touched my tongue, I knew this was no ordinary dinner roll. The surface was salty with a tangy buttermilk glaze, while the inside tasted as if a croissant had married a southern biscuit and had a baby: perfection.

Our host informed me that they came from a little bakery nearby called Victory to Agnes.

As it turned out, the bakery was only a couple of blocks away from my host's apartment, right in the heart of Greenwich Village. The next day I paid a visit to the unassuming storefront with its peeling red paint and frayed canvas awning to meet with the husband-and-wife team who started the bakery with the strange name.

Angus and Fiona Wolcott may be new to the neighborhood, but they are not new to baking. The couple moved their successful upstate bakery to Greenwich a little over a year ago when they decided that they wanted a safer place to raise a family.

Angus's hometown is Esther Wren, a small town in upstate New York with beautiful old homes, chintz-filled B&Bs, and artsy shops that sell beeswax candles and goat's milk soap. Not exactly the kind of place one would think would be unsafe to raise children.

"I've always found it amusing how people think of Esther Wren as a sweet little tourist town." Angus shakes his head as he makes a frothy Black Magic Latte for me. "But its origins are much darker than that."

Almost as dark as the origins of the deliciously rich Black Magic Latte? I wonder.

"It's a witch town," Angus tells me without breaking his focus as he draws a leaf into the milk foam.

Fiona joins us with a piece of cinnamon-ginger cake smothered in cream cheese frosting, a cake so dense and moist it takes only two forkfuls before you are full—yet somehow, you just can't help yourself from devouring it entirely. Must be witchcraft.

"People ask us all the time why our bakery is called Victory to Agnes. Most people joke that I spelled my name wrong."

But the real story behind the name is far more compelling. In 1982, when Angus was only seven, he witnessed a peculiar event that stayed with him.

"It was a witch fight. And it lasted for a little over two weeks," Angus tells me as he settles into the seat opposite me. "Actually, the fight had been simmering for years and years until one September when it suddenly escalated into full-out war. The witches lived next door to each other, so most of the action happened just two streets away from my house. People crowded the street at all hours. There were news crews, police, and fire trucks everywhere. My older brother, hoping to make a buck or two, sold T-shirts and buttons with opposing slogans: *Victory to Agnes* and *Victory to Millicent*—the names of the two warring witches."

"And judging by the name of your bakery, you sided with Agnes?" I say.

"Yeah. Most of my family and I sided with Agnes, mainly because she had red hair, and we redheads have to stick together. Except for my father. He rooted for Millicent, but that's because she was the pretty one. Well, that is until things got really ugly."

"Ugly?" I ask, half distracted by the maple pecan pie Fiona generously slices for us.

"Well, as I said, the fight began long before anyone was really paying much attention. It began with little things. Like with Millicent, who notoriously hated pink—one year, she even proposed that town council ban the color from the town—suddenly she started wearing pink everyday. Head-to-toe pink. She even had her hair dyed neon-punk-rocker pink. She painted her house pink, had her white Cadillac painted pink, and all her gardens stripped and replaced with only pink flowering plants. Then Agnes suddenly started wearing her undergarments on the outside of her clothes. We would see her at the grocery store shopping for butternut squash with her granny panties on display. In retaliation, she got Millicent to take up smoking.

"Rumor had it that she averaged five packs a day. She smoked herself gray. Later that spring, the deformities began."

"Deformities?" I ask, barely listening, as I'm now too busy focusing on the pastel-colored éclair trio that has been laid out before me.

"Millicent, the pretty one, suddenly went bald. Then, within a few months, her face completely changed—like *completely different person* changed. And not for the better. Rumor had it that Agnes grew a tail. But I never saw any evidence of that."

At this point, I began to choke on my éclair.

"I know, it sounds crazy. I feel crazy for even telling you."

"But what does all this have to do with baking?" I ask him, while trying not to choke on my éclair again.

"That September, a neighborhood kid was having a birthday, and instead of the usual pizza parlor, she decided to celebrate it in the middle of all the action. So we all piled into her mom's station wagon and parked on the street just outside of the witches' houses. It was a really hot day, and her dad set up a portable barbecue and we roasted hot dogs and drank grape soda and watched the vultures and ravens roost all over Millicent's house. During a lull in the action, her mother takes out a sheet cake from the cooler. It was chocolate with little orange and yellow sugar flowers, and it was the best cake that I've ever tasted. I knew right then and there that I wanted to be a baker. I've spent the last three years desperately trying to replicate that cake, and I think I've finally done it."

At that moment, Fiona appears once again with two square pieces of chocolate cake with orange and yellow flowers, served on paper plates with plastic forks.

"We call this Station Wagon Birthday Cake, circa 1982."

With my stomach almost bursting at the seams, I take a small bite and immediately swoon. Suddenly my appetite returns, and I finish the decadent cake with a few more bites.

With no room left to sample another cake or pastry, I thank my hosts for their hospitality. But I can't leave without knowing one thing.

"Who won?" I ask.

"Technically Millicent. Her house was left standing," Angus replies.

"Standing? What happened to the other house?"

"It blew up. Well, first it disappeared for like a month, and then, when it reappeared, it exploded. Gas leak apparently."

"And Agnes?"

Angus shrugged. "Not sure what happened to her. After her house blew up, it was rumored that she lived in a hydrangea bush in her backyard for a while, but I'm sure that was just an urban legend. Some people think that Agnes now works for Millicent, but I can't imagine how that would have happened. Millicent still lives in Esther Wren and sells real estate for a living. She sold our old place before we moved here. Got us a wicked deal too."

ACKNOWLEDGEMENTS

A very special thank you to my husband, John, who tolerates endless witch talk at the dinner table and to my parents who always encouraged me to follow my artistic path, even when as a teenager it led to a dark purple room and fire-engine red hair. I would also like to thank my sister-in-law Lynette and my assistant, Rebecca, who organize my daily life—making it possible for me to finish a painting or two. Thank you to Casey Decker from the Meticulous Type who first saw the potential for this book and to my editor, Elizabeth Kribs, and publisher, Tara Walker, who felt there was a place for me in fiction.

JANET HILL is a painter and children's book author/illustrator. Her work is both elegant and whimsical, and her painting style evokes a sense of nostalgia, mystery, and humor. Janet began her career in 2008 selling her original paintings on Etsy. Her online business has now grown to include a large range of art prints, cards, and stationery products. Her work has been featured in *Style at Home*, *Flow*, and *UPPERCASE* magazines, Anthropologie and has also appeared on *The Mindy Project* television show.

Janet has written and illustrated two picture books: *Miss Moon: Wise Words from a Dog Governess* and *Miss Mink: Life Lessons for a Cat Countess*. *Lucy Crisp and the Vanishing House* is her first novel. Janet lives in Stratford, Ontario, with her husband, John, the manager of an independent bookstore, and their dog, Atticus. Visit her at janethillstudio.com and follow her on Instagram @janethillstudio.